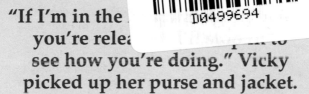

"If I'm in the _____ **you're relea**_____ **to see how you're doing."** Vicky picked up her purse and jacket.

The warmth of Chad's smile brought a ray of light to a portion of Vicky's heart that had been dark for a long time. How strange that she was here to help _him_, and he had encouraged _her_.

As Vicky walked down the hallway, she gradually lost the upbeat attitude she'd shown Chad. She had overheard a discussion in the hospital lounge not intended for her ears. She knew that Chad Reece was in for a sad awakening. When that happened, someone would have to be around to pick up the pieces, and maybe, just maybe, she would be that someone.

Books by Irene Brand

Love Inspired

Child of Her Heart
Heiress
To Love and Honor
A Groom to Come Home To
Tender Love
The Test of Love
Autumn's Awakening
Summer's Promise
*Love at Last
*Song of Her Heart
*The Christmas Children
*Second Chance at Love

*A Family for Christmas
  "The Gift of Family"
*Listen to Your Heart
Christmas in the Air
  "Snowbound Holiday"
A Husband for All Seasons
Made for Each Other

Love Inspired Suspense

Yuletide Peril
Yuletide Stalker
The Sound of Secrets

*The Mellow Years

IRENE BRAND

Writing has been a lifelong interest of this author, who says that she started her first novel when she was eleven years old and hasn't finished it yet. However, since 1984 she's published more than thirty contemporary and historical novels and three nonfiction titles. She started writing professionally in 1977 after she completed her master's degree in history at Marshall University. Irene taught in secondary public schools for twenty-three years, but retired in 1989 to devote herself to writing.

Consistent involvement in the activities of her local church has been a source of inspiration for Irene's work. Traveling with her husband, Rod, to all fifty states, and to thirty-two foreign countries has also inspired her writing. Irene is grateful to the many readers who have written to say that her inspiring stories and compelling portrayals of characters with strong faith have made a positive impression on their lives. You can write to her at P.O. Box 2770, Southside, WV 25187, or visit her website at www.irenebrand.com.

A Husband
for All Seasons

Irene Brand

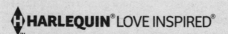

Recycling programs
for this product may
not exist in your area.

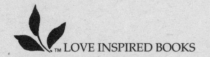 LOVE INSPIRED BOOKS

ISBN-13: 978-0-373-78866-8

A Husband for All Seasons

Copyright © 2007 by Irene Brand

www.Harlequin.com

Printed in U.S.A.

Then I heard the voice of the Lord saying,
"Whom shall I send? And who will go for us?"
And I said, "Here am I. Send me."
—*Isaiah* 6:8

Special thanks to my relatives Julia Pasquale, M.D. (specialty in emergency medicine), and Alice Giles, M.S. in nursing, for sharing their knowledge and experience about lacerations to the renal artery and subsequent kidney transplants.

Also my thanks to my friend Tony Leport, who steered me in the right direction for information regarding professional football players.

Chapter One

"Help! Help!"

Chad Reece struggled to open his eyes, wondering why he couldn't move. Was he lying on the gym floor with a heavy weight on his chest?

"Help!" a weak voice called again.

Chad was always the first to help when any of his teammates were injured. Responding to the distress call, he tried to sit up. Gentle hands on his shoulders pushed him backward.

"Don't try to move," a kind voice cautioned sternly. "You'll pull out your IVs if you don't settle down. I'm supposed to keep you quiet, so cooperate, please."

Chad opened his eyelids slightly, and even that was an effort. He wasn't lying on the floor. He wasn't in his apartment. He wasn't in his parents' home, so where was he? Who was this woman hovering over him—a woman, with a soft voice, who smoothed his pillow and wiped his face with a warm, moist cloth?

"Where am I?"

"You're in OSU Medical Center in Columbus, Ohio."

In the hospital? He never got sick—not since the ear infections he'd had as a toddler.

"Are you real? Or am I dreaming?"

"It isn't a dream, Mr. Reece. You were recently airlifted to the medical center from a small hospital in eastern Ohio. I don't know all the details, but it seems you had an injury that hospital couldn't handle. Don't worry—you're doing great. You've been calling for help, and I'm here if you need me. Go back to sleep."

Chad closed his eyes, but he didn't want to sleep. *Airlifted* to this hospital! The last he remembered, it was the first weekend in September, and he had been in Pittsburgh heading for the goalpost during the first football game of the season. He recalled the shouting of the spectators and the victory celebration of the cheerleaders—sounds that had been music to his ears since he had started playing football as a teenager.

When he had vaulted to safety with the ball, he must have grazed the goalpost, for it toppled and knocked him down. He had felt a sharp pain in his back, but that discomfort had faded into the background as they celebrated. He had scored for his team and started his third NFL season with a winning touchdown. Why worry about a pain in his back?

Eluding his many fans, at the end of the game, Chad got into his car, needing some solitude to unwind from the tension he'd been under for several days. After the emotional high of a game, nothing settled Chad more than driving alone through the rural area of Western Pennsylvania and Eastern Ohio. He didn't want to talk. He turned his cell phone off so he could concentrate on driving.

But a few hours of driving brought excruciating pain in his side and back. Although he was bent double with pain, he drove slowly to a hospital in the next town. He must have blacked out before he saw a doctor, for he didn't remember what happened after that.

Chad opened his eyes again. "And who are you?" he asked the aide, hardly recognizing his own voice, which sounded faraway.

"I'm Vicky Lanham, a hospital volunteer, and I'm sitting with you through the night. Your parents will be back tomorrow morning."

Parents? His parents were in Alabama. Although they had rarely missed any of his high school and college games, they had stopped following him when he turned pro. They had watched his last game on television. He must be having a nightmare.

He tried to sit up, but he couldn't move.

When Chad woke up again, he was more alert and aware of his surroundings. He was in a hospital, but the young woman had gone, and his parents stood beside his bed. Tears glistened on his mother's wrinkled, wistful face.

Trying to smile, he said, "Aw...it can't be that bad, Mom. What happened to me?"

She shook her head, unable to speak, and Chad turned questioning eyes toward his father.

"You had an accident at the football game. Don't you remember?"

"I remember Tommy and me bumping into each other and toppling the goalpost."

His father smiled wanly. "Yes, it was an outstanding victory at the last minute, thanks to you. But I wonder if the cost was worth it. You had to have surgery."

"Surgery? How long have I been in the hospital?"

"Five days. The doctor is coming soon to talk to us about your surgery and when you can be discharged."

Chad asked no more questions. He'd already learned more than he wanted to know. Besides his head hurt and he felt shaky inside, as if he had been sick for weeks instead of five days. He had never stayed overnight in the hospital, and he had been here almost a week! He was adopted, and although he didn't know anything about his birth parents, his pediatrician had always told him that he must have inherited good genes. And now he was in the hospital.

Chad closed his eyes, trying to sort out what his father had told him. If this had to happen, why couldn't it have been the last game of the season instead of the first? What if this surgery meant he couldn't play the rest of the season? He wished he could go back to sleep with the assurance that all he'd heard was a dream.

The surgeon came in a short time later, shook hands with Chad's parents and spoke cheerily to Chad. He was a slender, white-haired man with a gray mustache. An RN followed him carrying an electronic machine to record his condition. The surgeon checked all of the tubes and wires attached to Chad's body, and in a crisp voice, rattled off a lot of numbers and terms that didn't mean anything to Chad. The nurse logged the information into the machine she held since all the hospital's records were electronic.

Turning to Stewart Reece, the surgeon asked, "What have you told him?"

"Very little," Reece said.

"That's just as well, I suppose."

Chad became aware that his mother was crying softly, and he knew the prognosis must be serious. He steeled himself for bad news. Had he broken his hip when he had fallen? If so, he could kiss his professional football games goodbye for this season. Or a worse possibility—maybe forever.

Chad wondered at the compassionate expression in the surgeon's eyes as he turned toward him.

"Chad, your parents wanted to be here when I discussed your injury with you."

Mr. Reece moved to Chad's side and laid a comforting hand on his son's shoulder. Chad looked up at his father's face noting the signs of fatigue lingering in his eyes. Again it hit Chad just how old his parents were.

It couldn't have been easy for his parents to adopt a baby when they were nearing middle age. To Chad they'd often seemed more like his grandparents when compared to his friends' parents. Both of small stature, with fair complexions and blue eyes, it was obvious that the Reeces couldn't have borne a son as tall and muscular as Chad with his dark eyes and features. But there had never been a day when Chad hadn't loved them for giving him a home.

"We've kept you sedated for the past several days," the surgeon continued, "so you probably don't remember anything that happened. There isn't an easy way to tell you. You suffered a serious injury in that last ball game, but it must not have been apparent at first. You had taken a drive and stopped at a small hospital in Ohio. After a brief exam, it was obvious you needed more care than that hospital could provide. You were airlifted to OSU Medical Center because our surgical team is one of the best in the country for your type of injury."

He hesitated, and Chad, weary of the suspense, said crossly, "Well, what is it? What happened to me?"

"We're not certain if the goalpost fell on your side, or if your buddy's fall onto you caused your injury. Somehow you suffered a transverse process fracture of the thoracic spine and lacerated your renal artery."

"Say it in plain English, please?"

"Your kidney was crushed beyond repair."

Chad cringed from the impact of the doctor's words, but he had known when he started playing football that it was a dangerous sport. He swallowed with effort, trying to ignore the panic the doctor's words had generated. "Can't people live with only *one* kidney?"

"That's true," the surgeon agreed. "But that was the *only* kidney you had."

Chad turned a bewildered, frightened look on the doctor before his eyes darted toward his mother. So that's why she was crying! "I find that hard to believe," Chad said. "How could I have lived this long without two kidneys? It just isn't possible!"

"It is possible, but not common." the surgeon continued. "Some people are born with only one kidney and live perfectly normal lives. If you've never been to a hospital, there'd be no reason prior to this that your condition would have been found."

"I still can't believe it!" Chad argued, knowing that he didn't want to believe it.

The surgeon regarded him with gentle, compassionate eyes. "Chad, I've been a surgeon for more then twenty years. I've had at least ten patients, maybe more, who had only one kidney but didn't know it until something else happened to them and the abnormality was discovered when they were being tested for a different problem."

Chad closed his eyes, trying to take in this information.

"Also, I've removed countless diseased kidneys and my patients have lived out a normal life with only one kidney."

"Son, we had no idea about this," his father said. "Your health has always been good, and the problem didn't show up in the tests you took to qualify for football. I'm sorry we didn't learn about it sooner."

"You're not to blame." Looking at the doctor, Chad asked, "Does this mean I'm going to die if I don't have a kidney transplant?"

There was no fear in Chad's voice, and he tried to calm his racing pulse. Dying wasn't in his immediate plans for the future, but he had been a Christian since he was a boy, so he wasn't afraid to die.

"A donor was found rather quickly," the surgeon said. "We replaced your kidney yesterday, and you're doing great. Unless there are complications, which I don't expect, you can be released next week. You need rest more than anything else right now. The nurse has put a sedative in your IV, which will make you sleep."

He did feel sleepy, and Chad didn't protest when his parents said they would stay with him. His rest was troubled, and he felt as if he was weaving in and out of a fog. He had always believed that God held him in the hollow of His hand. If so, why had He allowed this accident to happen?

He had been playing football since he was

in middle school without any serious injuries. Why couldn't he have found out when he was a teenager that he wasn't normal? He'd always been so proud of his body, and all the time, he was an accident waiting to happen. Why did it have to happen now when his future was wrapped up in pro football?

Chad's hands moved restlessly and something tugged at the back of his mind and worried him. He finally woke up at the insistence of the woman he had seen the night before.

"What's your name?" he asked. "I forgot."

"Try to remember," she said. "You need to start remembering things."

"Are you a nurse?" he asked.

"No. I do volunteer work at the hospital, and sometimes I'm asked to sit with patients who shouldn't be left alone. I call a nurse if there's an emergency. Your parents stayed here with you until you were past the critical stage. Now that you're out of intensive care, they went to spend the night at a hotel to rest. I was asked to sit with you through the night."

He peered intently at her face, trying to remember her name. "Is it Vicky?"

She gave him a thumbs-up, a smile lighting her face. "Sure is. Vicky Lanham. Is there anything I can get for you?"

"I'm thirsty."

She poured a fresh glass of water, inserted a straw and bent it. She put her hand behind his neck and lifted until his lips touched the straw. The water soothed his parched throat and the touch of her cool hand on his warm skin was comforting.

She lowered his head to the pillow and picked up her purse and jacket.

"I have to go to work this afternoon, so I need to leave now."

"Are you coming back tonight?"

"You're getting along very well. You won't need any supervision that the nursing staff can't give you."

Chad closed his eyes, but opened them again quickly. The medication was making him sleepy, and he didn't want Vicky to leave before he thanked her. Blinking he said, "Thanks for helping Mom and Dad. I know they've been upset by all of this. The pain medicine they're giving me keeps me asleep so much of the time that I haven't really had much time to think about what a narrow escape I had. It seems like the doctors found a donor very quickly, but I've been so out of it when they were here that I haven't asked my parents if they know who it was."

"If I'm in the hospital again before you're released, I'll stop in to see how you're doing."

The warmth of his smile brought a ray of light to a portion of Vicky's heart that had been dark for a long time. How strange that she was here to help *him* and he had encouraged her.

As Vicky walked down the hallway, she lost the upbeat attitude she had displayed to Chad. Since his admittance to the hospital, scores of media representatives had been camped near the hospital waiting for the latest news about the football star. The surgeons had given daily reports of his condition and details of the serious injury were widespread. Seemed as if everyone in the nation, except Chad, knew what had happened to him.

Vicky had overheard a discussion in the hospital lounge not intended for her ears. She knew that Chad Reece was in for a sad awakening. When that happened someone would have to be around to pick up the pieces, and maybe, just maybe, she would be that someone. Up to this point, Vicky had drifted through life, but if she could help this man accept the disappointment he faced, it might provide a catalyst to deal with her own shattered dreams.

Chad woke from another nap when his parents entered the room, accompanied by his friend Lorene Saunders, carrying Amy, her two-year-old daughter. Chad stared when an orderly followed, pushing Perry Saunders in a wheelchair. Chad was speechless. In a few seconds he recalled his first meeting with Perry and Lorene several years ago.

He had met them before they were married, when he was a senior in college. That was the summer he had worked as a chauffeur and bodyguard for Jon Preston, his good friend and rising country music sensation. Chad had accompanied Jon to his gig in Woodston, Kentucky, where Perry was a professor at the local college. Lorene's public relations agency had been contacted to promote Woodston's bicentennial celebration. When she came to Kentucky to oversee the promotion, she and Perry were reunited for the first time in twenty years. Although they were twice his age, he had liked them at once, and they all became good friends. He was pleased when his parents also developed a liking for Perry and Lorene. The Saunderses later moved to Southern California, where Amy was born. After that, Chad saw them infrequently, although they talked often by phone.

"Regular old home week," he said. "Hi, Lorene. You're as beautiful as ever."

Lorene bit her curved lips as if she was trying to control tears that threatened to overflow.

Her long black eyelashes splayed over her face, and she didn't return Chad's greeting.

Dark circles bordered her blue eyes and it seemed that Lorene had aged since he had last seen her six months ago. But Amy's bright black eyes sparkled at Chad, and he believed the girl remembered him. He tried to lift his left hand to Amy's outstretched one, but his hand seemed as heavy as lead. He let it drop back on the sheet.

Chad's eyes scanned the four adults in the room. Did he imagine it or was there a guilty expression on their faces?

Attempting to believe that he was imagining things, Chad said, "It's good of you to come to visit me. But why are you in a wheelchair, Perry?"

Perry Saunders was the most handsome man Chad had ever seen. Tall and slender, with a well-proportioned body, Perry had black onyx eyes and thick silvery-gray hair. His trim mustache added dignity to his high cheekbones and straight, prominent nose. But a gray pallor marked his face today and his hands were trembling. Next to his father, Chad admired Perry above all men.

"I'm all right, Chad. I'll let your father explain."

Chad glanced toward his parents, but they

wouldn't meet his eyes. Without analyzing his feelings, anger welled up in Chad's chest.

"We've never hidden the fact that you were adopted," his father stated, a tremor in his voice.

"No. That's has never bothered me." But even as he spoke, in light of what he now suspected, Chad wondered if the statement was really true.

"We've known who your biological parents were for several years. We didn't tell you because you've always said you didn't want to know. But if it hadn't been for them, you might be dead now."

Again Chad glanced around the room. His suspicions were true, and he didn't like it. He didn't like it at all.

"I still don't want to know."

"Why, Chad? It seems so unusual," Lorene said. "Most people are curious about their family roots."

"I don't know exactly. I thought about it a lot when I was a boy, but as I grew older, it didn't seem to matter. Maybe I didn't want to admit that my birth parents didn't want me," he said, almost in a whisper.

Chad paused, and a chill seemed to have penetrated the room. The silence was deafening. Except for Amy, who was squirming in Lorene's arms, no one moved. Almost it seemed that no one breathed. After a suffocating moment, Mr. Reece cleared his throat.

"You'd always said that you didn't want to know, and frankly, we preferred it that way, too. I guess we wanted to feel that you were really ours. But when the surgeon said that your chances of recovery were low if you didn't have a replacement kidney right away, we had to choose between your life and letting you find out your roots. Sometimes it takes years to find a donor with a matching organ. We didn't want to lose you. We told your biological parents about your injury."

Breathing deeply, as if he found it hard to reveal the past after concealing it for so long, Mr. Reece said quietly, "As soon as Perry and Lorene heard from us, they boarded a plane immediately, either of them willing to be a donor."

Chad's gaze sharpened and he studied each of the adults individually. His mother had covered her face with her hands. Lorene's eyebrows had drawn together giving her face an agonized expression. Stewart Reece studied his son with curious intensity. A momentary look of pain crossed Perry's face, and a wistful plea for forgiveness shone in his eyes.

Chad turned his head and closed his eyes. His heart beat erratically. Learning about his bad injury was a bitter pill to swallow. He had told his parents that he didn't want to know anything about his origin, but surely after he met Perry and Lorene, he should have been told the truth. He felt betrayed, humiliated, and actually *stupid* that he hadn't even suspected who his parents were.

When he opened his eyes, the Reeces had gone. Perry had wheeled his chair close to the bed and Lorene stood beside him. Under Lorene's watchful eye, Amy was toddling around the room.

"We owe you an explanation, Chad," Perry said.

He shook his head, and he couldn't keep the tears from seeping under his eyelids. "I don't want to hear it."

He had idolized these two people. He didn't want to hear a sordid story that would topple them from the pedestal where he'd placed them.

"If you don't want to listen for yourself," Lorene said, "at least, for our sakes, let us tell you what happened. We've waited years to ask for your forgiveness."

"I don't want to hear it. Just leave me alone!"

"We are *not* leaving, Chad," Perry said in a voice that brooked no argument. "You need to hear the truth—after that, if you don't want to see us again, we won't bother you. But we've waited for years to explain what happened. You *are* going to listen."

Motioning to all of the tubes and medical equipment that held him immobile, Chad said bitterly, "I'm a captive audience, so I have no choice except to listen. But I promise you, I'm not going to like it."

Chapter Two

Dreading the upcoming exchange, Chad squeezed his eyelids tightly to stop further tears, hardening his heart against Lorene's pleading voice.

"The first time Perry and I had seen each other for over twenty years was in Woodston, Kentucky, where we first met you. We were college sweethearts who'd been engaged. Only *once* did we let our emotions get out of hand— the night you were conceived."

For the next half hour, Chad listened to the rich timbre of Perry's voice as he explained how through a misunderstanding and the stubborn conniving of Lorene's father, he never knew she was pregnant. Lorene thought that Perry had abandoned her and didn't love her. Perry was angry because he thought Lorene didn't want to marry him and had moved away without leaving a forwarding address. Because of these misconceptions, they didn't try to contact each other. They had remained unmarried because memories of the true love they had shared prevented them from having relationships with anyone else.

Every word they said was searing Chad's soul with the deepest agony he had ever known. His heart searched for an answer.

God, why didn't You let me die without hearing these things? I've always been happy. I had a good life. I'd rather be dead than to know that the four people I've loved the most have betrayed me. Why, God, why?

Their words were destroying one of Chad's fondest memories, and he wished they would stop talking and leave him with a few pleasant memories of their association.

"When you came to town with the Jon Preston group, we both suspected that you were our child for you looked exactly like Perry did at that age. Then we learned that you were adopted—and that your parents were the Reeces—and little doubt remained.

"Perry was determined to tell you that we were your parents, but I didn't think it was fair to the Reeces. I'd given you to them, and we agreed to say nothing. But the Reeces knew my name. And when we all met at your last college game, they knew who we were. They volunteered to let us share your life, and we've been grateful for that."

Through clenched teeth, Chad said, "Shouldn't I have had a say in that? I was old enough to make my own decisions. Was it right to treat me like a child?" Even as the words left his mouth, Chad realized he was acting childish now.

He heard Lorene's quick intake of breath, and he knew he had hurt her. Shattered by his own physical and emotional injuries, he had the desire to hurt someone else. If he lashed out at others, that might ease his own hurt.

But he didn't think he could ever forgive either set of parents for deceiving him.

In all fairness he had to admit he had always told the Reeces that he didn't want to know. So why did he suddenly feel as if the whole bottom had dropped out of his world?

He made no gesture to stop them as Lorene picked up Amy, and his biological family left the room.

Chad didn't see Perry or Lorene the next day, nor did Vicky Lanham show up as he had hoped. His parents spent the day in the room with him, but fortunately he dozed a lot. Apparently aware of his mood, they didn't force a conversation.

The surgeon came in late afternoon.

"You are doing great," he said, "and so isMr. Saunders. Your body is accepting the transplant remarkably well. There's no reason you can't live a perfectly normal life, if…" He paused and again Chad sensed deep compassion in the doctor's voice and eyes.

"If?" Chad prompted. "If what…?"

"If you give up contact sports," the doctor said bluntly.

"I'd rather die," Chad said without hesitation. "Football has been my life since I was a kid."

"I know," the surgeon said. "I've seen you play. You play with your whole heart, and I can understand how you feel. I know what it would mean to be told I could never perform another operation. I'm only telling you the truth. You might play out the rest of your NFL contract and never have another accident, but I doubt very much if the management will let you do it. Even if they wanted to, it's too great a risk, and probably no one would insure you." He squeezed Chad's hand. "I can't tell you how sorry I am."

The surgeon shook hands with Stewart and Betty, wagged his head sadly and left the room.

"Please go away," Chad said to his parents. "I don't want to talk to anyone now."

"I don't think you should be alone, son," Mr. Reece said. "Especially tonight. Let me stay with you."

"I don't want you to stay. I'm sorry, but I feel betrayed. If you had told me when I first met Perry and Lorene, it wouldn't have been so bad. But to let me go on without telling me is more than I can forgive right now."

"You shouldn't be alone," Mr. Reece insisted.

"Then ask the girl who has been sitting with me to come stay. I just can't be around the two of you right now."

Chad hated himself for hurting these two people who loved him and had given him a happy childhood. But to gain another set of parents and to lose his lifetime dream in less than two days was more than he could bear. *His parents.* Who were his parents in a case like this? Would Lorene and Perry expect him to call them Mom and Dad now?

But his heritage was a minor problem when he considered a future without football. What would he do without football? He had more money now than his parents had made in their entire life. He had invested his income wisely. He wouldn't have to work another day as long as he lived.

But what kind of future was that? He had always had something to do. He had started working when he was a boy—carrying newspapers and delivering groceries for the neighborhood store in Alabama where his father worked. In college, he couldn't have a job and play football, too, but he had worked out regularly in the gym and studied to make good grades. Not to mention the long hours of practice. No, Chad Reece, or should it be Saunders now—had never been a loafer.

And he didn't want to start now.

Vicky was surprised that she had been asked to sit with Chad again, and she dreaded seeing him. Chad had lots of fans on the staff of the hospital, and the word had spread like wildfire that his football days were over. How could she comfort him in the discouragement that must be eating at his spirit? She prayed she could help him, yet now that she was faced with the task, somehow it seemed so daunting.

She walked quietly into Chad's room. A large arrangement of roses from his team's managers and coaches dominated the nightstand, and the room smelled like a greenhouse. The light over the bed was off, but the hall light shed a dismal reflection around the room. There was enough light to see Chad lying with his hand over his forehead, half shielding his eyes. Tears trickled in tiny rivulets over his face. The injury had been sustained such a short time ago, and to look at his muscular body no one would suspect that he had had such a serious operation.

Vicky watched him for several minutes. Her face flushed when she realized she was spying and that Chad probably wouldn't want her to see his tears. She backed out of the room, knocked and reentered. He hadn't changed at all. Knowing he was awake, she went to the bed and touched the hand that lay across his brow.

He seemed to know instinctively who it was. Without opening his eyes, he said, "I'm not asleep. Thanks for helping out. I'm doing great, physically, but my parents insisted that I should have someone with me, and I didn't want them. I'm out of sorts with them at the present."

Vicky laughed lightly as she put down the tote she carried, took off her denim jacket and hung it over the back of the chair placed close to his bed.

"I understand that. I get out of sorts with my mom and dad sometimes, too."

"If I could go to sleep and forget about it, I'd be happier, but I've slept a lot today. Besides my head is spinning with all of the things I've heard in the past few hours."

She lifted his bed slightly and put a pillow

behind his shoulders. She held a glass of water to his mouth and he took a few sips through the straw. She sat beside him.

"If you want to talk, I'll be happy to listen. If you clear your mind you can probably go to sleep."

With a slight grin, Chad said, "Well, you asked for it." He hesitated, not knowing if he was willing to share his newfound knowledge with anyone. Still it would be easier for him to talk to a stranger—someone he probably wouldn't see again.

"I've known as long as I can remember that I was an adopted kid, and I didn't mind at all. That is, until today when I learned that I've known my biological parents for a few years—have been good friends with them—but didn't suspect who they were."

"And that bothers you?"

"Perhaps it shouldn't, but I must have been naive not to have suspected it before. My biological father is my kidney donor. My adoptive parents contacted him as soon as they knew how serious my condition was. He and my 'real' mother came right away."

"Why does that upset you?"

"I don't know," he said. Then sighed. "I suppose I'm mad at myself because I hadn't suspected before. My mother said that she suspected I was her son immediately because I look like my father. And it's true. I feel like I should have noticed my physical resemblance to Perry long ago. I was really rotten to both sets of parents, and that bothers me more than anything else. And I'm not normally…like that."

"I'm sure they understand. You've had a shocking experience, not only physically, but emotionally as well. No one expects you to act like nothing has happened."

Now that he'd started talking, he couldn't seem to stop. "I've never doubted that it was God's will for me to play football. Now I wonder how I got the wrong direction. My dad didn't want me to play football, but when I was so determined to play, he didn't discourage me. That's one reason I love my parents so much— they always put my welfare before their own. They adopted me because they wanted a child. Up to now, they haven't had any reason to regret it, but I feel like I let them down today." He sighed again. "It's not easy managing anger and guilt at the same time."

"It will work out, Chad," Vicky said, realizing that she had used his first name, but he didn't seem to notice. "Maybe it *was* God's will for you to play football for a while. He may have other plans for you now."

"Do you really believe that? I mean, has that been true in your life?"

Vicky squirmed uncomfortably in her chair, thankful that the lights were dim in the room so Chad couldn't see her expression. His problem and doubts had touched a sensitive place in her heart. At one time, she knew without any doubt God's will for her life. But she had gotten sidetracked. She and Chad had more in common than he knew. Of course, her injury was an emotional one. She thought fleetingly that if she told him about her hang-ups it might give Chad a lift.

"I've had problems with my directions, too, but they're not as fresh in my mind as yours are. You talk tonight and I'll listen."

Chad talked most of the night about his childhood. The early years in his parents' home. The summer he had worked with the Jon Preston band and had met Lorene and Perry in a small Kentucky town. He had been drawn to them immediately, never dreaming they were his parents.

"After they moved to California, I didn't see them often, but we kept in touch by telephone and email. All of that time, my parents…" he paused and in the dim light, Vicky saw pain cross his face "…didn't give any indication of my heritage, nor did Perry or Lorene."

"I have a feeling that none of your parents will expect you to change your relationship with them. I'm sure the Saunders won't expect you to start calling them Mom and Dad. If they've kept the secret of your birth from you all of these years, they won't expect any more from you than you're willing to give."

"They tried to talk to me, but I brushed them off."

"That's understandable. I know you're not asking for advice, but why don't you come to terms with your injury and the change in your future before you concern yourself with your family relationship?"

Chad seemed not to have heard for he continued, "I should be grateful that Perry donated the kidney and saved my life. But that's hard to do when I wish I had died. I'm only twenty-five and my usefulness on earth is finished. Anything will certainly be better than what I'll face in the next few years. I've heard of too many professional athletes who lost all sense of purpose and headed down the wrong road when they couldn't keep playing."

In an effort to steer his mind to more pleasant thoughts, Vicky said, "I'm sure you have some pleasant memories of the time you've spent with your biological parents."

With a slight smile, he said, "The best thing

is that I now have a little sister. Amy was about six months old when I first saw her, and it was a case of love at first site for both of us. Lorene says that she's always been shy with men, but she came to me right away. Maybe she sensed we were related. She's a cutie! I hope you can see her."

He moved restlessly in bed. Vicky stood and straightened the sheets and gave him another drink of water.

"When are they going to take all of this hardware off of my arms so I can do something for myself?" he complained.

"It won't be much longer," Vicky said soothingly. She put another pillow under his shoulders and spread a blanket over the sheets.

"Is that more comfortable?"

"Yes, thank you. I'm sorry for being such a grouch."

"You aren't being grouchy. Do you think you can sleep now?"

"I'll try. You won't leave?"

"Not until my shift is over. I'll wake you before I go."

Vicky could easily understand why Chad preferred to have a stranger with him during this trauma rather than some member of his family.

As Chad slept, she unwillingly recalled the

most embarrassing time in her life. What she had done hadn't been so terrible—she'd only fallen in love with the wrong man. A man several years her senior, already engaged to someone else. Vicky remembered as if it had been yesterday, when she and her friend, Amelia Stone, had been sitting in a church service in flood-ravaged Williamson, West Virginia.

She had wanted to enter full-time Christian service, and her parents had always been strong supporters of the Red Cross. They had encouraged her to volunteer to help in the flood cleanup, suggesting the hands-on work with hurting people would give her insight into whether a humanitarian profession was the way for her to go.

The experience had not turned out as they had hoped. Vicky had developed a huge crush on Allen Chambers, the pastor of a local church, whose members loaned their church for the Red Cross headquarters. But when the minister had announced the name of his fiancée from the pulpit and introduced her to his congregation, Vicky was devastated because she had made no effort to conceal her love, or perhaps her infatuation, from Allen. She thought he returned her affection, but she soon realized that the minister had never suspected that she had a crush on him.

She and Amelia had left the church before the service was over so she wouldn't have to face Allen again. She had avoided any contact with him during the days she remained in the area to help the Red Cross. But the incident had destroyed Vicky's self-confidence. She cringed inwardly when she recalled that a subsequent incident had also destroyed her self-esteem.

Feeling rejected by the young minister, Vicky had returned home from the flood disaster, doubting that God had called her to serve Him by working in foreign countries as a missionary. She had disappointed her parents by leaving college after the first semester, even though they lived only a few blocks from Ohio State University.

She hadn't expected them to support her. She moved into an apartment and started working in a bookstore at a minimum-wage salary. She was living from hand to mouth, doing very little worthwhile except volunteering at the hospital and participating in activities at her local church.

Although she had tried to kill her dream of serving others, Vicky's mind often turned in that direction. That was one reason she had started volunteering at the hospital. God wouldn't let her forget the vow she had made to Him in a church meeting when she was fifteen, dedicating her life to full-time Christian service.

Vicky took a Bible out of her tote bag and turned to the fifth chapter of the book of Ecclesiastes and considered the words of Solomon. As always when she read the passage she felt condemned because she hadn't kept her vow.

Do not be quick with your mouth, do not be hasty in your heart to utter anything before God... When you make a vow to God, do not delay in fulfilling it... It is better not to make a vow and not fulfill it... And do not protest to the temple messenger, "My vow was a mistake."

Had *her* vow been a mistake? Had she acted on her emotions rather than waiting until God spoke to her heart? But if God hadn't called her, why couldn't she forget that electrifying moment when she felt as if He had singled her out for some particular mission? Did God ever allow a person to forget His call? Or did He cause the person to be uncomfortable until she fulfilled His will in her life?

Because a purposeless future loomed before her, Vicky could empathize with Chad. Was she going to spend her whole life without any sense of direction? At the end of her life, would she have anything to show that she had really lived?

Suddenly, Vicky had a feeling similar to the one she had experienced when she thought she had been called to the mission field. Was God really dealing with her heart again? What else could it be? Chad groaned in his sleep, and she quickly put the Bible away and stepped to his side. She checked the equipment and everything seemed normal.

Vicky's heartbeat accelerated and she wondered if God was sending her a message that He hadn't cast her aside. She was suddenly overwhelmed with the enormity of the rehabilitation that Chad would need as he dealt with the loss of his profession. She could understand why he was angry over the unwanted revelation of his illegitimate birth. Could it possibly be that her mission in life would be to help Chad Reece take his place in a world that didn't include football?

"Oh, no, God," Vicky whispered, and she quickly surveyed the handsome youth before her. "I make too many mistakes when it comes to matters of the heart. Not only once, but twice, I've really messed up. I can't bear to think that I'd risk my heart again."

Could she be the friend that Chad needed in

this stressful time without succumbing to his personal magnetism?

Although she didn't necessarily believe that God spoke audibly to His followers in this current day, she knew that He did speak through His Word. She opened the Bible again to the book of Ecclesiastes, and as she read the familiar King James Version, she recalled a more modern version of another passage.

Two are better than one, because they have a good return for their work: If one falls down, his friend can help him up. But pity the man who falls and has no one to help him get up!

God, she prayed, *if I can be helpful in lifting Chad Reece from his depression, I'm available.*

Chad was still sleeping when it was time for Vicky to leave, and she hesitated to disturb him, but she had promised. She touched his arm lightly, and he stirred.

"Chad," she said, "I'm leaving now."

His eyes opened reluctantly. "I didn't think I'd go to sleep."

"How do you feel?"

"Too soon to tell, but the pain seems better. My mind is still fuzzy. I hope they take me off some of this medication today—I'm not used to it. Will I see you tonight?"

She shook her head. "I have to work tonight, and you don't need anyone." She held up a piece of paper. "I've written down my cell phone number and the number at work. Please call me if you need me to help you. If I have reason to be in the hospital before you leave, I'll stop by to see you."

"Thanks for helping me," he said.

Vicky walked down the hall thoughtfully, wondering if she would see Chad again. His home was in Alabama, and the Saunders's lived in California. He would probably go to one of those places to recuperate. He had no ties with Ohio, so he probably wouldn't return. But her recent experience in God's presence caused her to believe that their paths *would* cross again.

His new kidney was operating as if it had always been in his body, and on the surgeon's next visit, Chad was told to expect a full recovery. By noon, Chad had been set free from all of the machines, IVs and tubes that had kept him in bed. A nurse helped him into a wheelchair, and he ate his lunch sitting up. He was weak and still on pain medication, but he accepted the fact that he was going to get well.

He should be overjoyed, but in his frame of mind, it really didn't matter.

"You can be discharged in a few days," the surgeon had told him. "Since Columbus isn't your home, I can send your records to a competent hospital in whatever region you move to. I want you to return here in three or four months for a checkup, but your recovery and therapy can be done elsewhere."

The Reeces came in while the surgeon was still in the room, and he reported directly to them. "You can take him home with you, by plane, in two weeks. I'll check out an adequate hospital in your area where he can be treated as necessary."

After the surgeon left, Mr. Reece said, "Lorene and Perry have suggested that you might want to go with them to California. It will be all right with us if you want to do that. They're closer to a large hospital than we are."

"How is Perry doing?"

"As well as you are," his mother said. "You are fortunate that he was available and willing to be a donor. They plan to go home the first of next week."

"Your agent is also in town," Stewart said. "He tried to come into the hospital to see you, but the surgeon has banned all visitors except family, and the receptionists know that there are only five of us here. He wants you to call him as soon as possible."

Chad had no desire to talk to Howard Crayton, his agent. He had always been outgoing, loved people and made friends wherever he went. At this point, the life of a hermit appealed to him. Perry was a quiet, more reserved person than Chad had ever been. Had he taken on more of his father's personality than he knew? Or had the trauma of the injury and consequent transplant made him want to avoid people?

"When Howie calls again, tell him that I don't want to talk to him now and that he should leave Columbus. When I'm ready, I'll call *him*. As for going home with you, I don't want to do that, either. And I won't go to California. I have some difficult decisions to make and I want to be alone to make them. I intend to stay in Columbus until the surgeon releases me completely."

Chad realized that he had spoken more bluntly than was his nature when Betty gasped. "This isn't like you, son."

Chad stretched out his hand and Mrs. Reece placed her trembling fingers in his grasp. "Nothing about this situation is *like* me. I don't want to hurt you, Mom, but you're used to having me gone. I believe it's better for my health to stay here for a few months. I have to sort out my life now—I can manage better alone."

He lifted his mother's hand and kissed it.

"Are you still mad at us for not telling you?" she asked.

"No, not mad, just embarrassed because I was too naive to see the truth for myself." Turning to his father, Chad said, "Go on home. You have your interests there. I'll find an apartment close to the hospital and will be perfectly all right. I'm used to being on my own now."

"What about your apartment in Pittsburgh? And your car is still in the hospital parking lot in Ohio."

"My apartment is paid up for the year and my housekeeper checks on it occasionally when I'm away. My car is leased, so I'll get in touch with the company and have them pick it up. If I stay here long, I'll lease another car." Still holding his mother's hand, he said, "It will be all right. I'll come out of this a better man than I've ever been. Don't worry."

They crept out of the room like wounded, reprimanded children, and Chad hated to see them go like that. It was troubling to think that he might never feel the same way about them again. His family loyalties were going to be different whether or not he wanted them to be.

Chapter Three

Two days later, lying in his hospital bed, Chad heard a plane overhead that had apparently just lifted off from Columbus International Airport. The oval face of the clock on the wall opposite his bed registered the hour his parents' plane should be leaving for Alabama, and he hoped they were on their way home. He breathed deeply, thankful for their understanding that he needed to be alone.

But he squirmed uncomfortably and a sense of inadequacy alarmed him when he realized how ill-equipped he was to deal with his biological parents. Neither Perry nor Lorene had come to see him since the day they'd discussed his birth with him. No doubt they were unsure of their welcome. Although he dreaded talking to Perry and Lorene, he would have liked to have seen more of Amy. She had become the most important person in his life, and he always felt like he was ten feet tall when she climbed on his lap, gave him a slobbery kiss, and said, "Chaddie, I lub you." One of the nurses had told Chad this morning that Perry would be released soon, and he couldn't let them go without making the effort of reconciliation.

He rang for a nurse to find out the number of Perry's room, which was at the end of the same hall Chad was in. The nurse helped him put a robe around the hospital gown he still wore, and she walked beside him to Perry's room.

"Please ring when you want to return to your room. The doctor wants us to watch you closely for a few more days."

The door was ajar and Chad's hand trembled as he lifted it to knock. Perry's deep voice called, "Come in."

Lorene and Amy were in the room, too, and he was glad to find the three of them together.

Perry was reclining in bed, entertaining Amy who sat beside him playing with a doll. Lorene was leaning back in the upholstered chair with her eyes closed.

"Why, Chad!" Perry spoke happily. "Come in."

Lorene's eyes popped open and she stood at

once, started toward him, her face radiant, but checked herself.

"You look wonderful," she said.

"That's the way I feel, thanks to Perry." He turned to his biological father. "And you must be doing all right, too. The nurse told me you're scheduled to be discharged soon."

"Yes. Our plane leaves at one o'clock tomorrow."

"We'd like for you to go home with us. You and Perry could go to the same hospital for monitoring. It would mean a lot to us," Lorene concluded slowly.

"I realize that, but I'll tell you the same thing I told Mom and Dad. I have to sort out my future, and right now I can do that better alone. I'll stay in Columbus for a while. I'll try to come and visit you after that. I don't know."

Lorene's lips parted in protest and Perry shook his head at her.

"We accept that. When you're ready to talk, we'll be waiting. Our past behavior doesn't give us any right to interfere with your plans. We'll be grateful for any part of your life you want to share with us. We don't expect you to think of us as your parents, but we hope we can continue to be your friends."

"I hope so, too," Chad assured them in an

apologetic tone. "It's just that I'm a different person than I was two weeks ago."

Lorene's dark eyes searched his face, apparently looking for something she didn't see. "Do you think you can ever forgive us?"

"I don't know," he said after a heart-wrenching pause. "I don't know," he repeated softly. His body trembled, whether from weakness or tension, he wasn't sure. But Perry must have noticed.

"We're grateful that you visited us today, but we won't try to see you again before we leave, so let's pray together." He held out his hand. Chad took it and then picked up Amy's tiny fingers, while Lorene took her place on the other side, gripping tightly the hand of her husband. Amy's fingers wiggled under Chad's touch, and he experienced a sense of belonging he had never known before.

"God," Perry prayed. "None of us are the same as we were a few weeks ago, but we're thankful that You never change. We are made in Your image. You breathed into us a living soul, which belongs to You eternally. For some reason You have upset Chad's life, but I believe You still have great plans for him. Many people can play football, but there's something that only he can do for You. Take control of his future as You have his past and help his parents and us to accept all of his decisions as Your will. Thank You for allowing me the privilege to give him life two times. Amen."

Chad's throat was too tight to say anything and unshed tears stung his eyes. He squeezed Perry's hand before he released it to bend over the bed and give Amy a hug. He circled the bed and gathered Lorene into a warm embrace. He held her close for a few seconds before he turned and left the room, scurrying down the hallway as fast as he could, forgetting until he reached his room that he was supposed to call a nurse to accompany him.

Expecting to enter his room and crash emotionally, Chad cringed when he saw the man sitting beside his bed. *Howard Crayton!*

Bending an angry glance upon his agent, Chad demanded, "How did you get in here?"

Howard, a short, slender, wiry individual, vaulted out of the chair as if he was on a spring. He extended his hand.

"Meet your elder brother," he said.

It took a few seconds for that comment to register, but when it did, Chad demanded angrily, "Did you sneak in here pretending to be my brother? Didn't Dad tell you that I don't want to talk now?"

"That he did, old buddy, but I've got offers for you that will far exceed your fondest dreams. Opportunities that would make a mummy want to talk."

Chad's hands shook, and he didn't know whether the trembling was caused by weakness or anger.

"I've been searching around for ways to capitalize on your injury. You might get offers for endorsements. You're the talk of the nation right now. I couldn't wait to share this with you. We're going to get rich, Chad."

Stifling his anger, Chad leaned against the wall to support his trembling body. He wasn't as strong as he had thought.

"Since you barged in here uninvited, sit down. If you remember there's a clause in our contract stipulating that either of us can sever our association with a week's notice. Forget capitalizing on my injury. It's something I want to forget. I *will not* make any decisions until I can sort out what I think is best for me. If you don't leave Columbus immediately, your one week's notice starts today."

Howard's face took on a sickly pallor, and he dropped into the chair, deflated as a punctured balloon. "You can't do that! Not after all I've done for you," he said cautiously.

"What you've done for *me!* Do you have any other client who's made as much money for you as I have?"

"Well…no."

"I'm not emotionally competent to make any major decisions right now. I may get in touch with you in a few weeks, but it might be a year. I don't know."

"Yeah, man," Howard said. "I got carried away with all the possibilities opening up for you, rather than thinking of all the doors that are closing. Sorry. I'll take a plane out of here tonight."

Although Chad had complained about spending a week in bed, the morning's emotional trauma had drained him and bed looked good to him. He kicked off his slippers and stretched out on top of the sheets. He rested physically, but his mind was still active. What should he do now? Since he was being released from the hospital soon, he needed a place to live. He would have to stay in a hotel for a few days until he had time to find an apartment. Perhaps Vicky Lanham could give him some information about available apartments.

He had been airlifted to Columbus from eastern Ohio in a hospital gown and wrapped in a blanket. Fortunately his mother had bought him two sets of clothes before she left town. Once he was released in a few days, he could buy some more things. Then, after he was settled, he could call his housekeeper and ask her to ship his fall and winter clothes to him, if he decided to stay in Columbus.

The day before he was to be released from the hospital, Chad called the number Vicky had given him. Feeling fortunate to reach her on the first try, he said, "I'm going to be discharged tomorrow, but I intend to stay in Columbus for the time being. Do you have any suggestions about an apartment for rent?"

Vicky's heart beat a little faster at his call and a warm glow flowed through her. Maybe God *was* giving her another opportunity to do His will.

"Give me time to ask some questions, and I'm sure I can suggest something. Is anyone picking you up tomorrow?"

"No, my parents are gone now. I'll take a cab to a hotel and stay there until I find a place to live."

"Actually, I don't have to work tomorrow. I've got a car, so why don't I pick you up and take you to a hotel? By that time, I may have located some vacant apartments for you to check out."

"I shouldn't impose on you. I can take a cab."

"When will you be released?"

"Tomorrow morning, but I don't know the time."

"Your surgeon usually makes his rounds early, so I'll guess midmorning. Stay put until I get there. Okay?"

"Okay," Chad agreed, laughing. At this point, he could accept help from Vicky easier than from his own family.

When Vicky arrived at the hospital the next day, Chad was waiting in the lobby in a wheelchair. He wore navy-blue sweats, with an OSU ball cap perched jauntily on his head, a gift from the nurses who'd served him. No one would guess by looking at him that he had recently had a serious injury and a delicate operation. His firm and generous lips widened into a smile when he saw Vicky.

An orderly wheeled Chad to her car. He had to flex his long legs to fit into the front seat of her compact car. Vicky tossed the plastic bag holding his possessions into the backseat.

As she drove away from the hospital, Chad looked with interest at the majestic university buildings. Strangely enough, although he had been wishing he had died, it was good to breathe the fresh air and to feel the warmth of the sun on his face as it shone through the car window.

"It's hard to believe that a month ago, my life was all figured out," he said. "I thought I would be playing pro football for years. Now

I'm at loose ends, hardly knowing what to do. I have an engineering degree, although I may have to take some refresher courses to catch up with changes in the field. My dad supported my dream of playing football, but he insisted that I train for a profession when my career was over. I couldn't see much reason for it, but I guess he knew best."

"You don't *know* that you can't play football, do you?" she queried in her soft, sweet voice.

"I haven't talked to any league officials yet, but the surgeon advised against it. If I don't hear anything within a few days, I'll call, but I want to put off hearing the official's decision as long as possible."

While she drove, she found herself wishing that she could have known Chad before this injury messed up his life.

"I have a reservation at the University Plaza Hotel," he said.

"That's a good choice and close by. And I may have found an apartment for you. Do you want to check it out before you go to the hotel? It's expensive, but I'm guessing that probably isn't an issue with you."

"I'm used to a simple lifestyle, so I'm not interested in anything too fancy."

"Why don't I drive by and let you look at the house and the neighborhood? It's located in a

Victorian home on Neil Avenue, not too far from the university. It's a handy location for appointments at the hospital."

"If you have the time, I'd like to see it."

"When I was looking for an apartment for myself, I looked at this particular space, but it was too pricey for me. I met the landlady then, and was thrilled when I called and found out it was vacant again."

"If we come to a bank before then, will you pull into an ATM so I can withdraw some cash? Fortunately, my wallet and other items I had in my pockets were sent to the OSU medical center with me."

Vicky pulled into a branch bank and Chad withdrew five hundred dollars. She drove along High Street, where many of the businesses catered to college students. The street was congested, not only with vehicles, but with pedestrians, all with backpacks, heading for their classes.

Intent on her driving, Vicky kept her eyes straight ahead, which gave Chad an opportunity to watch her. He hadn't really looked at Vicky at the hospital. *Too intent on my own problems,* he thought.

Tall and graceful, Vicky was worth a second look, although all he had noticed about her in the hospital were her compassionate, heavily lashed blue eyes. Now, he admired her brown hair tumbling to her shoulders in soft curly waves. Her smooth ivory skin glowed with rose undertones. She had a gentle but overwhelming beauty, and he was surprised he hadn't noticed it before.

He didn't want Vicky to catch him watching her, so when she took a right off High Street and drove to Neil Avenue, Chad turned his attention to the century-old houses.

The street was lined with large trees, and their foliage was a mixture of yellows, reds and greens. Chad was amazed at the change in the foliage since he'd entered the hospital. The football season had just been starting then, but the hint of fall was evident in the fading flowers and the occasional fallen leaves drifting downward to the street.

Constructed of brick and stone, most of the houses had three floors. He especially liked the rounded turrets on many of the residences.

He listened to Vicky's comments as he squirmed uncomfortably in the limited space of her car.

"Several blocks of these houses were renovated a few years ago. The area is called Victorian Village. Some of the houses are one-family dwellings, but several have been turned into apartment buildings. I live in an apartment two blocks to the west."

Vicky pulled over to the curb before a red-brick dwelling with a one-story stone porch across the front. A wide doorway was centered on the porch. A sign in front of the house indicated an apartment was for rent.

"The apartment is on the second floor of that house. The owner couldn't afford the upkeep and taxes on the property after her husband died, so she had to rent part of the house or sell it. There's only one apartment in this house, so you wouldn't be bothered with a lot of noise."

She pointed to a roofed stairway on the left side of the building. "That's a private entrance to the apartment."

"Do you suppose we could see it now?" he asked.

"We can ring the doorbell and find out if the landlady is at home."

Vicky was out of the car and had opened his door before Chad had time to ease his body out of the vehicle.

He grinned up at her as she stood by the car's open door. "I've never had a chauffeur before. I might have to give you a permanent job."

"You'd better hire someone with a bigger car," she answered. "I'll push that seat backward before we leave here to give you more legroom."

Vicky timed her steps to his slower gait, but climbed the front steps before him and turned the old-fashioned bell in the center of the front door.

A woman opened the door on the first ring. She was a tall, bony woman probably in her sixties. She had piercing, blue eyes, and her straight, iron-gray hair was cut short. She nodded to Vicky, apparently recognizing her, and then she turned questioning eyes on Chad.

"I called yesterday about your apartment. Would it be convenient for us to look at it now?" Vicky asked.

"You married?" the woman said, glancing from one to the other.

The comment discomfited Vicky, but before she could answer, Chad said, "No, ma'am. I'm the one who needs to rent an apartment. Vicky lives a few blocks from here."

"Just checking," the proprietor said. "I won't have unmarried people living together in my house."

"That suits me," Chad said.

Mrs. Lashley had the reputation of being a plainspoken woman, but Vicky hadn't expected such candor from her.

"Mrs. Lashley," Vicky said. "This is Chad Reece—he's from out of town."

She nodded. "I could tell that from his slow, Southern drawl."

Striving to hide her amusement, Vicky continued, "He's been in OSU hospital and he needs a place to stay while he recuperates. He wants to be close to the hospital until his surgeon releases him."

"I won't take a lease for less than a year."

Thinking that Mrs. Lashley didn't need to rent the apartment as much as Vicky thought, Chad said, "If that's the case, we won't take any more of your time. I don't know how long I'll be staying. Thank you. Let's go, Vicky."

Mrs. Lashley followed them out on the porch, and they were halfway down the short walk when she said, "Well, I could lease it for six months."

Chad turned and smiled. "Let me look at the apartment."

Mrs. Lashley stood aside and they entered a wide entryway that ran the length of the residence. Coming inside out of brilliant sunlight, they were plunged into semidarkness. Wooden shutters covered windows that were curtained with white lace panels. Mrs. Lashley flipped a switch and a chandelier spread light on the stairway to the left of the hall. She walked sprightly up the wide walnut treads. Chad counted thirteen steps as he held on to the sturdy, carved handrail and slowly followed Mrs. Lashley and Vicky to the second floor.

"The apartment only takes up half of this floor," Mrs. Lashley explained. "I have a daughter and grandchildren who visit from time to time. I keep the other rooms for them."

At the top of the stairs, the hallway extended the length of the house as it did on the first floor. The two rooms on the left had been turned into a comfortable apartment, and Chad thought at once that it was the kind of retreat he needed. A partition divided one of the rooms into a bedroom and a bathroom with a claw-foot tub, a shower stall, a large marble pedestal sink and a toilet. The other room was a combination living room and dining area, with a small kitchenette off to the side. The rooms were sparsely furnished, but they suited Chad's present needs.

Chad asked the price, which was less than his Pittsburgh apartment. Motioning Vicky to one side, he asked, "What do you think of it?"

A flash of humor crossed her face. "I'd snap it up in a hurry if I could afford it. You won't find anything better than this unless you want to move into an expensive condo."

He shook his head. "No, I think this will suit me just fine."

He turned to Mrs. Lashley. "I'll lease the apartment, and if I leave before the six months is over, I'll pay you the full amount." She had stipulated that he would need to pay two hundred dollars to hold the apartment until she checked his references. He took the money from his wallet and handed it to her and gave her the names of his lawyer, his accountant and his pastor in Pittsburgh.

"I'll call in a few days to see when I can move in."

Driving away from the Lashley home, Vicky said, "You made a good choice. The rooms are comfortable, and you'll have an interesting landlady."

Chuckling, Chad commented, "She seems that way. And this location will be perfect for my needs. The doctor doesn't want me to drive until I see him again, so there's no need to rent a car. But they told me at the hospital that the bus service is good, so I can explore Columbus while I recuperate."

"The Lanham Taxi Service operates daily, too," she suggested with a sly grin in his direction.

"I figure I'll be calling on that service often, but I'll try not to make a nuisance of myself."

Vicky had learned the hard way not to push her company on a man, so when she left Chad at the hotel, she didn't make any comment about seeing him again. Any overtures of friendship would have to come from him. She didn't look back as she drove away.

Chapter Four

After three days of loneliness, anxiety and indecision, Chad finally called the manager of his NFL team.

"How are you, Chad?" the manager asked. "Your father notified us when you were released from the hospital, but he didn't have a phone number for you."

"I didn't feel like talking when I was in the hospital and I've only been released a few days. And thanks for the roses—they sure brightened up the room."

"We wanted you to know we were thinking about you."

"Well, what's the bad news?" Chad asked, pacing the floor but trying to sound nonchalant. "I think I know, but I'll make it easy on you and ask."

The man hesitated, and the seconds seemed

like hours to Chad. "It's the hardest decision I've ever had to make in my life, but we have no choice except to release you from your contract."

Bile rose in Chad's mouth, and he felt as if a mule had kicked him in the stomach. He had feared this decision was inevitable, but hearing it from the manager's mouth drove the final nail in the coffin of his dead hopes. He wasn't a crybaby, so he forced himself to say cheerfully, "Well, it was a great life while it lasted. And I'm thankful that you guys gave me the opportunity."

"I've never understood why bad things happen to good people, but somewhere down the road, we'll know the answer."

"That may be true," Chad said, and he couldn't hide the bitterness in his voice. "But I'm going to need some answers before I regain the unquestioning faith I used to have."

Chad laid aside the phone and leaned against the wall. He couldn't even envision a life without football. But now that he knew with finality that he would never play pro ball again, he had to come to terms with the future. He paced the floor of the room, annoyed because he kept dwelling on his bad fortune rather than on the many things he had going for him.

Financially Chad was worth several million dollars so his livelihood was no problem, but he wasn't comfortable with so much money. He was heavily insured, so no doubt the expensive surgery wouldn't cost him anything. And if he remembered, the insurance company would be responsible for compensation for several months after his operation. His father managed a grocery store, and his mother had stayed home to look after her son. They couldn't afford any luxuries for themselves or for Chad. If he wanted anything extra he had to make the money to buy it. How well he remembered his teen years when he had worked one whole summer to earn enough money to buy a bicycle! Then he received his NFL signing bonus. Suddenly, he was rich.

Instead of going on a spending spree, he went to a reputable investment broker for advice. He invested the majority of his signing bonus. He put a million dollars in an account for his parents, enabling Mr. Reece to retire from the store with a good income over and above his Social Security. Chad's lifestyle didn't change that much. He knew what was important in life—and it wasn't material possessions.

He made more money on his investments than he ever spent. So why couldn't he be thankful that he had no financial worries instead of fretting over his disrupted plans? In twenty-five years he'd had more opportunities than most people did in a lifetime. So what was his problem?

He could find work without any trouble. But was it right for him to take a job that another man probably needed to support his family? Would it be more charitable to invest his money in a business that would employ other people? There were lots of questions, Chad decided, but no satisfactory answers.

One major question filtered through Chad's mind. After it seemed that God had offered him life on a silver platter, why was it suddenly snatched away? Was he mad at God? Chad feared that this was the root of his present dissatisfaction. Even admitting the possibility of such an attitude lowered his self-esteem and Chad's faith was stretched to the breaking point. This was an issue that could only be settled between him and God.

In the meantime, he had a life to live. He called a taxi and rode into the center of Columbus's business district on High Street. He got out of the cab in front of the capitol, wondering why the dome was so stubby. Had the founding fathers of the state run out of money before they completed the dome? He sat on the stone wall that surrounded the capitol's lawn, watching and listening to the steady drone of traffic along the city's main thoroughfare.

After living for two years in Pittsburgh, Chad still wasn't accustomed to big cities. His small Alabama town could be set down in the space occupied by Columbus's large financial district, but he didn't feel as crowded here as he did in most cities. Chad felt no urge to do anything, but eventually he stirred, walked a half block and crossed the street.

He went into a bank—the same corporation that he used in Pittsburgh and arranged for a transfer of funds.

From an ATM machine, he withdrew some cash for his immediate needs. He walked a block to a department store, using his credit card, purchased a jacket, two knit shirts, slacks, a pair of dress shoes, heavy socks and running shoes. With the sweats and the underwear his mother had purchased, he could manage until he decided what to do with his personal things in Pittsburgh.

He caught a taxi back to his hotel, where he found a message waiting from Mrs. Lashley. He could move into the apartment at his convenience. Seeing no reason to pay another night's hotel bill, Chad dialed Vicky's number.

When three days passed, and Vicky hadn't heard from Chad, she started wondering if she would ever see him again. She didn't recognize the number on her Caller ID when the phone rang.

"Hello," Chad said. "Is the Lanham Taxi Service operating today?"

"It is until noon when the proprietor has to go to work." She laughed. "Where do you want to go?"

"To my apartment. Mrs. Lashley left word that it's ready."

"I'll pick you up in an hour. Can you be packed by then?"

"I'm packed. I bought some new things today, and they're still in the plastic bags. I bought a duffel bag for my other clothes."

"What about bathroom and kitchen supplies? Since you probably don't feel up to shopping, I'll pick up some towels, soap and other things you'll need. I'll get some bread and milk for you, too."

His cheerful laugh thrilled Vicky. It was a good sign that he was starting to heal emotionally as well as physically. "I hadn't given that any thought. My housekeeper kept my Pittsburgh apartment supplied, but I intend to get along without a housekeeper now. It would be great of you to buy those things. I appreciate it."

"Okay. Then I'll see you soon."

Vicky had been moping around for several

days, but the surge of adrenaline she received after Chad's call turned her into a dynamo. She quickly gathered the things she would need for work and hurried out to the car.

"God," she whispered before she turned the ignition key. "Am I really getting the opportunity to help Chad Reece? He's a famous, wealthy man, and when he's well again, he'll probably go back to his old friends and forget all about me. I must not expect more from him than he's willing to give."

Was God calling her to serve Chad? She started to think this might be so when the tense expression on Chad's handsome face relaxed into a smile when he saw her.

With an answering smile, she asked, "Anybody looking for a taxi?"

"Yes, one poor vagrant."

"Let's go then." She picked up his duffel bag. "I'd better take this."

"It embarrasses me to have you carrying the heavy items, but I think the duffel bag weighs more than I'm allowed to lift for another week."

During the short drive to Neil Avenue, Chad told her about the call from his manager and about his shopping trip during the morning. After he got the key from his landlady, she helped him upstairs with his luggage and the supplies she'd bought for him, then said, "I've got to go now."

"I don't even know where you work. I've spent too much time talking about myself, rather than listening to you."

"I work in a bookstore on High Street near the OSU campus. My parents think I'm wasting my time, and I guess I am, but I make enough to pay the rent, my food and gasoline. That's all I want now."

"Will you be finished in time to have dinner with me tonight?"

"That depends on what time you want to eat. I work until seven o'clock."

"That's all right with me. Will you drive by and pick me up? I don't know the town yet. You choose a restaurant. I'll be watching for you just blow the horn."

Vicky would have preferred to go home and shower before she picked Chad up for dinner, but she didn't want to keep him waiting. She went to the restroom and checked her appearance in the mirror on the door before she left the store.

She wore a pair of knit pull-on black pants and a light pink sweatshirt with a white collar. Not very dressy, but at least the color of the shirt complemented her creamy skin and brought out the rosy tint of her cheeks. She pulled a comb through her hair, hitched her bag over her shoulder and hurried out to the parking lot. Chad was sitting on the porch banister waiting for her when she reached his apartment house.

He was dressed in a white knit skirt and black trousers, and Vicky was pleased. Having left his casual clothes behind might indicate that Chad was looking forward instead of backward.

She chose a family-type restaurant not far from their apartments. From talking to Chad's parents, and also from his own comments, she knew that, in spite of his rise to fame in professional sports, he still had the simple tastes of an Alabama boy who had grown up in a small town atmosphere.

A waiter showed them to a corner booth and took their beverage orders. Chad commented on the antique cooking and farm implements arranged on high shelves around the ceiling. "Reminds me of home," he said.

Vicky noted the wistful look in his eyes and knew that he wasn't as relaxed and cheerful as he seemed. When the waitress arrived with their glasses of iced tea, she ordered a pasta salad.

"I really like the pasta dishes here," she said

to Chad, "but all of the food is good." To the waitress, she added, "And I want a piece of French silk pie for dessert."

"I have an appetite today, the first time since I had the accident." He ordered a steak, baked potato and some broccoli florets in cheese sauce.

While he was deciding on a salad, Vicky said, "This restaurant is noted for its coleslaw."

"I'll take a side of that, too," he told the waitress. While they sipped on tea, Chad said, "I'll have to be careful of what I eat. Now that I won't be going to the gym every day, it will probably be easy for me to gain a lot of weight."

"How much do you weigh now?"

"I've tried to stay at two hundred pounds. I'm quicker on my feet at that weight." Thoughtfully, he added, "I've often wondered if I might get heavier in middle age as many men do, but now that I know Perry is my biological father, I don't think I will. At least, I'll be happy if I look like he does when I'm his age."

"You will," Vicky assured him.

"I suppose I'm already healing," he said. "It doesn't hurt me to face the fact that he's my father now."

"You had too many traumatic things hurled at you in a short time. Now that you're healing physically, your emotions will shape up, too."

"But what about you? You hinted that you understood how I felt because you'd had a similar experience. You listened to me. It's your turn now."

Vicky hesitated. How could she confide in Chad? She believed he had a good opinion of her now, and she didn't want to change that.

"It really isn't much compared to what you've faced. I'd just as soon not talk about it now. Tell me about your life in Alabama. I've lived in Columbus all of my life, and I don't know much about small town life."

"You haven't traveled much?"

"No. I have relatives who live in Florida, but they usually come here to visit us. The longest I've been away from home was when I volunteered for Red Cross duty in southern West Virginia during a bad flood. I thought when I was growing up that God had called me into a life of service and that seemed a good way to find out if I had the right stuff to be a missionary."

"I was a Boy Scout and I helped in southern Louisiana after a hurricane once. What I saw there showed me how fortunate I was. What incidents made an impression on you?"

As Vicky related how she had watched her coworker, Amelia Stone, rescue a stranded child from an overflowing creek, Chad realized what a wonderful companion Vicky was.

Vicky paused, puzzled by Chad's intent stare. At his sudden question, she wondered if he'd been listening to her flood adventures at all.

"I suppose I should have considered this before I invited you out for dinner, but are you dating anyone?"

"No, not now."

"Good. I suddenly realized that I might be causing you a problem by asking you to spend so much time with me. I'm not dating anyone, either. Since I turned pro I've been cautious about women. Too many athletes are set up for compromising situations and get sued. I've avoided that by not keeping company with anyone."

Vicky concealed her amusement, but she wondered why he didn't consider her a threat. Didn't she exhibit enough femininity to attract him? Then again, that suited her just fine. She had been burned twice in relationships and she didn't want any more involvement. Finding out how Chad felt, she concluded that her decision to let him take the leadership in their companionship was a wise one.

They enjoyed a leisurely dinner, chatting about their high school years. Vicky found

Chad easy to talk to, and when she took him home, he said, "I've enjoyed the evening. Let's do this again soon."

"All right," she said lightly. "Give me a call. The Lanham Taxi Service aims to please."

Chad settled into his new apartment and within a few days he felt at home. Although he wasn't much of a cook, he existed on what he could prepare. He had no communication with his landlady. She apparently confined her activities to the first floor.

Chad was lonely, because he had always had lots of friends, but he didn't want any company now—an attitude that didn't make any sense even to him. He changed his cell phone number and hadn't given it to anyone except Vicky, and she didn't call, although he hoped that she would.

After a week, he contacted his parents and Lorene and Perry to give them his phone number, but he didn't tell them where he lived.

"Please don't give my phone number to anyone," he told both sets of parents. "As long as you don't know where I am, you can easily stall anyone who's trying to get in touch with me."

His father answered in a tone of voice that Chad had seldom heard from him. He was plainly annoyed with his son's attitude. "We're getting lots of calls that we can't very well ignore without being rude. Your teammates have been calling almost every day, asking about you and wanting your phone number. Tommy is nearly frantic because he blames himself for your injury. You should call him, at least. You can't hide forever, Chad. If you go to the hospital for checkups, someone is going to find you."

"Maybe, but I'm going to enjoy being an ordinary person as long as I can."

After a week of solitude, Chad was much stronger. His incision rarely bothered him, and he went to the rehab center of the hospital and worked out on the easier machines. The surgeon had advised him to avoid strenuous exercise for several weeks, but he couldn't stay inactive. He was fed up with his solitary life.

He started exploring Columbus on foot. At the break of day, he left the apartment and walked toward the business district. Within a week he had no difficulty walking four or five miles each morning. After his walks he stopped at his favorite coffeehouse on High Street for breakfast.

Chad called his housekeeper in Pittsburgh and asked her to send his casual clothes and a few of his suits. On the first day of November, he awakened, looked at the calendar and knew he had to face reality. He rented a box at the nearest postal branch and notified the post office in Pittsburgh to forward his mail to it.

He waited several days before he stopped at the post office on one of his morning walks. Expecting to have some mail, he was surprised to see only one card when he bent down to peer into the box. The card indicated that he should call at the window for his mail.

He handed the card to the clerk. She looked at the card and scanned his face with interested, amused eyes. She obviously knew who he was.

With a sly grin, she said, "Did you bring a truck?"

"What do you mean?"

She motioned to three large cloth bags behind the counter. "They're full of mail forwarded from Pittsburgh. You can take your mail in the bags, if you'll return them."

His amazement must have shown on his face, because the clerk couldn't control her burst of laughter.

"It's been less than two months since I picked up my mail. How could so much have accumulated in that time?"

"You're a popular man," she said, apparently enjoying his discomfiture.

The bags obviously weighed more than he

should lift. "Do you have someone to carry them to the street for me? I'll have to call a cab."

"No problem, Mr. Reece. I'll call the cab and tell the driver to come to the loading dock in the back. You can wait out there. Just follow the sidewalk to the rear of the building. We'll load the bags on a cart and bring them out for you."

When the cabdriver hopped out of the vehicle to load the bags for him and asked, "Where to, Mr. Reece?" Chad gave him the address on Neil Avenue, knowing his whereabouts would soon be common knowledge. The man chatted about Chad's football career all the way to his apartment. Although still hesitant to face his changed status in society, Chad responded to the man's comments on his past glory.

The cabbie carried the bags up the stairs and into Chad's apartment and piled them in a corner.

"Will you dump the contents of the bags into the garbage bags and take these cloth bags back to the post office for me?"

"Glad to do it, Mr. Reece. You know, I never thought I'd meet you face-to-face."

The driver's mouth parted in a wide smile when Chad shook hands with him and gave him a generous tip. He handed Chad a busi-

ness card. "Here's my number—call me anytime you need a cab."

Chad knelt and spread the mail. Among the
ever-present junk mail, he saw envelopes that
must contain get-well cards and personal letters. It would take weeks for him to open and
read the mail.

Chad frowned in desperation as he stared
down at the massive pile. He couldn't deal with
it today. He picked up his phone and dialed
Vicky's number.

She answered immediately.

"Did I catch you at home?"

"No," she said. "I'm in the grocery store. I
stopped on my way home from work."

"Will you be free for dinner this evening?"

"I always go to church on Wednesday nights.
But I don't work at all tomorrow."

"Then let's spend the day together. I plan
to lease a car tomorrow so I can pick you up."

"Would you like to go to church with me tonight?" Vicky asked.

"I probably should, but I'm not quite ready
to deal with crowds yet. Thanks for asking."

"Then I'll see you tomorrow. I'll walk to
your apartment. What time?"

"Why don't I call you after I have the car?"

"Good. That will give me time to do my
laundry."

* * *

Chad leased a blue, medium-priced car the next day that wouldn't attract attention. He telephoned Vicky, and before ten o'clock, he parked in front of her apartment house. He didn't know which apartment was Vicky's, so he waited for her to come out.

The sky was a bright blue with a few fleecy clouds making a pleasant contrast. The temperature was in the midseventies. The trees bordering the street had lost most of their leaves. Chad lowered the window and breathed deeply of the air that held a tint of wood smoke. God had created such a beautiful world for mankind to enjoy that Chad found it difficult to be downhearted today. And when Vicky strolled toward him wearing a denim suit and a blue blouse that matched her eyes, he thought that a pretty girl could go a long way to cheer a man up.

He got out of the car and opened the door for her.

She admired the shiny blue car and the ivory interior.

"Pretty neat car," she said.

"I don't know whether it pays to lease a car or not," he said, "but since I've been playing for the NFL, I've done most of my traveling by plane. I've never owned a car. When I was at home, I rode a bicycle or borrowed Dad's car. Now that I won't be on the football circuit, I may decide to buy one."

He settled in the car beside her. "Where do you want to go?"

"I'm just going along for the ride," she said. "What do you want to do?"

"I thought we might get out of the city and drive around. I don't know anything about Ohio. You may think you won't be doing anything, but you're the guide. I'm going to buy your lunch, and maybe even dinner, if we're out long enough, so you have to do something to earn it."

She looked at him with amused wonder, marveling that his state of mind had improved considerably since she had met him.

"I hear you! Let's take I-270 until we get to Route 62 and go northeast on that until we reach Holmes County. We can eat our lunch there and take another route returning. If that's too much driving for you, I can drive while you rest."

"Sounds like a good plan to me," he said, and he followed her directions to find the road she had indicated. He drove leisurely for almost two hours enjoying the beautiful, well-kept, productive farms and comparing them to the less fertile soil of Alabama.

They stopped for lunch in Berlin at an Amish restaurant. After one look at the vast varieties and amount of food on the buffet, Chad said, "I'm not to be trusted at this kind of spread. I'll order from the menu, but you choose buffet if you prefer."

"This restaurant is known for its potato soup," she continued as the waitress took them to a table. "I'll settle for a large bowl of soup and a piece of their famous apple pie à la mode."

When the waitress offered them a menu, he shook his head. "Bring us two bowls of potato soup for now. And I want unsweetened iced tea." He glanced at Vicky. "What do you want to drink?"

"Water with lemon for now. I'll have hot tea with my apple pie later."

He took a deep breath and slouched in his chair.

"You're tired," Vicky said. "I shouldn't have let you drive so far. Why don't I drive home and you can enjoy the view?"

"Sounds good to me. It irritates me when I wear out so quickly."

He marveled that Vicky could talk about his disability without seeming to "fuss" over him as his mother did.

"You seem to be more adjusted to the change

in your life. Or are you putting on a front for me? You don't have to, you know."

"No, I'm not adjusted," he admitted. "Sometimes in the night I wake up so angry that I can't stand myself. I've gotten up a few times, dressed and walked up and down the street."

"That might not be wise. Columbus isn't as safe as an Alabama town."

"I know that, but when I get in those moods, I don't care what happens to me."

"Been there and done that," Vicky admitted, "but you should consider the thousands of people who admire you and *do* care what happens to you."

Shamefaced, he said, "I do feel guilty about my thoughts. I shouldn't have told you but so far, you're the only one I dare let down my guard for. I feel kinda mean, as if I'm using you, but as long as I'm honest about it, you can tell me if you get tired of being a sounding board."

"I don't mind at all. Honestly, you're helping me, too. I've not accomplished a great deal in my life, and if I feel I'm of any help to you, it lifts my self-esteem considerably."

As they ate their meal, Vicky contemplated the risk she was taking. When the day came that Chad no longer needed her and could find his way alone, what would *that* do to her self-esteem? She felt sure that God had a great future in store for Chad. And when he finally overcame his disappointment and realized that, God would open up opportunities that would take him a long way from Columbus, Ohio. She would have no place in that new life.

"I am making some progress, though," Chad said, interrupting her thoughts. "I recently rented a box at the post office and picked up my mail yesterday."

With enjoyment he told her about the large amount of mail that had been forwarded to his box. "It will take *days* for me to sort through all of it. If you have any extra time, maybe you can help me with that?"

"It's only midafternoon. We could work on it the rest of the day as far as I'm concerned."

"Why don't we do that? I don't want to get in bad with my landlady by entertaining you in my room, so I'll ask her to play chaperone."

"Do you think she will?"

"I have no idea. I rarely see her. But I'll convince her that we are friends and nothing more."

Although she knew it shouldn't matter, his comment left Vicky with a hollow feeling inside. He obviously didn't share her feelings. Was she making *another* romantic mistake?

Chapter Five

Nothing he had done since his injury had brought Chad the peace and satisfaction as this day of traveling through rural Ohio with Vicky. He hadn't realized that he had dozed until she reached the Interstate to take them to downtown Columbus and the car's speed increased.

He sat up from his slouched position and yawned.

"I'm sorry I haven't been very good company. Have I been asleep very long?"

"Maybe a half hour. You needed the rest. Don't worry about it."

She stopped in front of his apartment twenty minutes later. "If you'll wait a minute, I'll check and see what Mrs. Lashley thinks of our plan," he said.

Chad walked up the front steps and rang the doorbell. Considering the speed with which

Mrs. Lashley opened the door, he wondered how much time she spent looking out the window.

After greeting her pleasantly, he said, "I wonder if you have time to help me for a few hours."

She lifted her eyebrows, eyeing him suspiciously.

"My mail has been forwarded and I have three large bags that have to be sorted. I'd like for Vicky to help me, but since I know you're concerned about the reputation of your home, would you mind helping us? I'll pay you for your time."

"Mr. Reece!" she said, a frown spreading across her face. "I'm not in the habit of charging for favors to people. Unlock the door into the hallway, and I'll be up shortly."

As he returned to Vicky, he wondered if his landlady was smothering a smile or did he just imagine it?

He was grinning widely when he opened the car door. "Drive around to the back of the house and park. The formidable Mrs. Lashley has agreed to keep an eye on us."

They were sitting on the floor with the contents of one of the bags spread around them when she entered the room.

"Make yourself at home, Mrs. Lashley," Chad said.

"If I'm 'at home', I need to be working. What can I do?"

"You know your way around the apartment," he said. "It would be super if you'd pour us some ginger ale. And there's a bag of cookies in the cabinet."

She marched into the kitchen and Chad heard doors opening and closing. "You don't have much to eat in here, young man," she called.

Chad favored Vicky with a lopsided grin and whispered, "Just what I need—*another* mother when I already have *two*."

"You can tell by looking at me that I'm a light eater," Chad answered his landlady.

"Humph." Her answer sounded loud and clear from the kitchen.

Mrs. Lashley soon brought in two cold drinks and put them on the floor beside Vicky and Chad with a napkin underneath. Vicky judged that she was probably in her early seventies but she was as spry as a puppy.

"Don't spill that on the carpet," she warned as she set a plate of cookies before them.

Mrs. Lashley had a cloth tucked under her arm and she started dusting the furniture.

"Young man," she started, and Chad interrupted her.

"I have a name, you know. Why not call me Chad?"

She acquiesced with a slight nod. "You should dust this apartment and run the sweeper. There's a sweeper in the pantry. Haven't you found it?"

Chad winked when he caught Vicky's eye. "I haven't looked. I'm not much of a house-keeper."

"Then I'll have to come in weekly and give these rooms a once-over."

Shaking her head, the landlady took the magazines and newspapers Chad had left on the coffee table and put them on a bookshelf. She looked into the bedroom and sighed.

"Bachelors!" she muttered.

By the time she had cleaned the apartment to her satisfaction, Vicky and Chad had sorted the contents of one bag into three stacks: first class, junk mail, and questionable.

"I can't make any decision on what you want to keep," Vicky said. "But if you'll toss me the things you want to dispose of, I can stuff them into this garbage bag we've emptied."

Mrs. Lashley sat on the couch and watched Vicky and Chad for several minutes. "I'll be glad to help," she said.

"You can help Vicky unload and sort the second bag while I check through this first-class mail," Chad said. "But I mustn't impose on your good nature."

"Assuming that I have a good nature," she said as she pulled a stool close to where Vicky sat on the floor.

Noting her twinkling blue eyes, Chad said, "You're not fooling me, Mrs. Lashley. Beneath that gruff exterior, you're a lovable teddy bear."

"Humph! Don't try my patience, or you'll find out. And you don't need to call me Mrs. Lashley. My name is Grace."

So Chad had won over Mrs. Lashley as quickly as he had her, Vicky thought as she sorted the mail and Chad and Mrs. Lashley quibbled about nothing in particular. What was there about Chad Reece that made him so personable? Vicky thanked God that his real personality was overcoming the tragedy in his life. But she wondered again if Chad was putting on this carefree front to hide the misery he felt inside. If so, that wasn't a good thing, and she eyed Chad carefully while they worked. She decided that for the present he'd forgotten about his tragedy.

After sitting and scooting around on the floor for a few hours, Chad had difficulty standing, and Vicky noticed that he clapped his hand on his back. Was his incision bothering him?

They had filled two garbage bags with junk mail, which Vicky carried downstairs to the garbage pails. But the living room floor still looked as if a hurricane had struck, leaving paper and debris in its wake.

"I've had enough of this for today," he said. "It will take several days for me to answer these or to decide if I want to answer them. I guess I'll have to buy, or rent, a laptop computer and a printer."

"You surely don't intend to leave the room in this condition," Grace said, her eyebrows lifting dramatically.

"Yes, I do. I'm not expecting company except the two of you, and since you've helped make this mess, no need to hide it from you. I'm hungry. Let's order a pizza."

"Humph." She threw her hands wide in dismay, "Well, you're paying rent on the apartment. You don't need to order any pizza for me. I'll go downstairs and eat my dinner."

"You'll do nothing of the kind," Chad said. "I insist that you eat with us—that is, if you like pizza."

Vicky assumed that Grace had realized that she and Chad weren't romantically involved or she wouldn't suggest leaving them alone in the apartment.

"I do like pizza, and I'll eat with you, but

I want to contribute my bit to the meal. I just happened to make an apple pie this morning. We can have that for dessert."

"Then I'll order pizza and salads."

Vicky looked into the kitchen. "I see you have a coffeemaker. I'll make a pot of coffee to eat with the pie."

Grace was back with the pie by the time the pizza and salad was delivered. They gathered around the kitchen table and Chad prayed a blessing over their food. Everything seemed cozy—like home. As Grace and Vicky discussed news of Columbus, Chad realized why he felt so comfortable. Neither of the women seemed to be treating him differently because he was injured. And that was one reason he didn't want to be around others—even his parents. He couldn't stand to have people feeling sorry for him. Was that why he was shutting everyone out? He had never been ill—never had been in a situation where he was an object of pity.

Even if he had analyzed his hang-ups about his injury, he still wasn't ready to become a public figure again. It was ten o'clock by the time they finished eating and had put away the dinner dishes. Grace wrapped the leftover pizza in aluminum foil and put a plastic cover over the pie.

"I'll leave this for you for tomorrow," she said. "I'm going home now. I don't keep late hours like you young people. Just give me a call when I can help again. It's kinda nice to have young people in the house. My daughter hasn't lived at home since she graduated from OSU. She married and moved to Texas. I only see her once or twice a year."

She left the room and closed the hall door behind her, so Vicky knew that she and Chad had passed muster with his landlady. Chad dropped his super genial air almost as soon as Grace left the room. He motioned Vicky to the couch and he sat in the lounge chair and pulled the lever to lift his feet. He looked tired and he made no effort to hide it from her.

"Grace turned out to be a very nice person after all."

Chad nodded. "For several hours, I forgot that my life had changed at all. You and Grace are good for me. I'm healing, but I'm not ready yet to see many people. Could you suggest a place where I could be alone for a couple of weeks? Maybe a state park where I could camp and no one would know me?"

"We have several nice parks not far from Columbus. But you've been in the news a lot the past month. Your picture, as well as clips from your football games, have been on local

TV. If you want to avoid people, you may need to conceal your real name."

"You're probably right." He motioned to his mail. "Some of those letters are from people who want to make a movie about my life or publish a biography. Several are job offers. And a manufacturer of football equipment wants me to sponsor their products. I had supposed that I would be a 'has-been,' but it looks as if my injury has made me a hero. I don't know how to deal with it. Does it seem odd that I want to be alone?"

"Not to me, it doesn't. I have to work tomorrow, but let's plan to check out some of the recreation areas and parks nearby on Sunday afternoon."

"That suits me."

"Will you go to church with me Sunday morning?" She asked hesitantly.

He paused for several minutes before responding, "Yes, I will."

"If you're willing to face a congregation of believers, you've passed your first hurdle," she assured him with a tremulous smile.

Chad drove Vicky home and walked up the steps with her. At her apartment door, he said, "What time should I pick you up Sunday?"

"If we go to the early service, it won't be so

crowded. Pick me up at nine o'clock so we can make the 9:30 service."

He bent forward and planted a kiss on her forehead. "Thanks for today."

Chad thought he would be ready for sleep after such a strenuous day and he went to bed as soon as he returned to the apartment. But he couldn't fall asleep, and after an hour of turning from one side to the other, he sat up in bed and piled pillows behind his back. He turned on the television, but none of the shows interested him. He was tempted to call Lorene and Perry. With the three-hour time difference, they wouldn't be in bed yet. He should at least check to see if Perry was still doing all right, but until he could regain some semblance of his "old" self, he didn't want to talk to them.

He heard an occasional car travel along Neil Avenue, and he got out of bed and walked to the double windows that commanded a view of the street. Through the leafless maple trees in front of the house, he saw pedestrians as well as automobiles. A couple strolled along the sidewalk, walking several small dogs on leashes. He got dressed, put on his running shoes, went down the steps and walked until he was physically spent.

He fell across the bed without undressing again and slept until daylight.

* * *

One corner of Chad's mouth lifted in a smile when she got into the car on Sunday morning, but Vicky noticed that his expression was tight with strain. Was it caused by pain or emotional stress?

"Good morning," she said cheerfully, hoping to dispel some of the gloom that seemed to hover around him.

"It is a good morning," he agreed, "but I haven't slept much the last two nights and I'm feeling sluggish. I'll get over it. How far is your church?"

"About a twenty-minute drive. When I was a teenager, my family went to a smaller church when we lived in the country. We started going to a mega church when we moved into the suburbs."

Accustomed to a small church building, Chad was amazed at the size of the church complex that must have covered ten acres of ground.

"There's a school, too, so they need a large plot of land," Vicky explained as she directed him to a convenient parking space.

Sensing Chad's need for privacy, she had intentionally arrived a few minutes late for the service. They entered the large auditorium through a side entrance into a small alcove during the opening hymn. They could easily see the preacher and the choir but were hidden from most of the congregation.

Chad sang a pleasing baritone, which he thought complemented Vicky's strong alto voice. Their voices blended harmoniously as they held the same hymnal. The warmth of Vicky's fingers helped ease his tension when they occasionally touched his hand. In spite of his uncertain future, he was glad to be in church again. Because of his varied NFL schedule, he hadn't joined a church fellowship in Pittsburgh, and his church attendance had been sporadic. Although this was a huge organization compared to his church in Alabama, he felt at ease.

Dressed in a suit, instead of a robe, the minister took his place behind the lectern. After greeting the worshippers, he read his text from the book of Proverbs. "If you falter in times of trouble, how small is your strength."

Chad felt as if his spirit had been stabbed with a knife. If he didn't know it was impossible, he could easily believe that the preacher had known he would be in the congregation and that he'd prepared the sermon especially for him. The preacher *hadn't* known, but *God* knew he would be there, and Chad listened intently.

The sermon focused on the life of Job and the many troubles he had endured. During the loss of his family, his wealth and his health, Job's faith had remained strong. In the midst of his trials, the ancient patriarch had been able to say, "But He knows the way that I take. When He has tested me, I will come forth as gold."

Was God testing him? Compared to what Job had faced, Chad's troubles were minimal. Then why couldn't he be man enough to stand up to his difficulties with the kind of faith that Job had exemplified? The minister closed his message with another challenging verse from the Bible, "We walk by faith not by sight."

Was his faith small? He was worrying about what to do with the future. He was struggling over forgiving his parents. No wonder the minister's closing verse from the New Testament seared his conscience and his heart.

They left the church through the entrance that led to the parking lot and Vicky thought she had been successful in avoiding anyone who might want to detain Chad. She groaned inwardly when she saw her parents bearing down on them. They didn't know that she had been helping Chad.

"Wait up, Vicky," her mother called.

"Hi, Mom, Dad. I want you to meet Chad Reece. I met him in the hospital and invited him to church." With an apologetic glance at Chad, she said, "My parents, Steve and Rachel Lanham."

Her father stepped forward eagerly and extended his right hand to Chad. "This is a pleasure, Chad. I'm a fan—I like your style."

"Thank you," Chad said, finding it wasn't as difficult to meet people as he had thought.

Rachel Lanham greeted Chad with a smile, and he saw that Vicky had gotten her good looks from her mother. Mr. Lanham was a burly sort of guy who wouldn't stand out in a crowd, but Chad took to him right away, as if he'd always known him.

"Are you coming for lunch today?" Rachel asked Vicky.

"Not today."

"I was expecting you." Turning to Chad, Rachel said, "And we'd like you to come, too— that is, if you like meat loaf."

"I do like meat loaf, but I'll take a rain check on the invitation, if that's all right."

Chad wondered at the tension he sensed between Vicky and her parents as she turned and walked to her car. "I'll come for lunch next Sunday, Mom."

"You, too, Chad?" Steve called after them.

"I'm not sure what I'll be doing next week. But thanks."

Chapter Six

As they walked toward his car, Chad said, "I had intended to take you to lunch, but it's fine if you want to eat with your parents instead."

"No, I've planned the day with you and I've already prepared our lunch." Her brows lifted inquiringly. "Unless you're afraid of my cooking."

Chad enjoyed her gentle camaraderie, knowing that Vicky's friendship had contributed largely to the slow healing he was experiencing. "I'll risk it. After eating just cheese, peanut butter and crackers most of the time, I'm not choosy."

"Actually, it's a picnic lunch. When I heard the weather forecast and learned how warm it would be today, I put together some sandwiches. Let's drive by my apartment and pick up the food. If it's okay with you, we'll go to one of the parks I mentioned and eat there. But it will be a couple hours before we get to the park. So if you're hungry we can go to a restaurant for lunch and picnic later."

"I had breakfast rather late this morning, and my appetite still isn't back to normal. I'd rather drive for a while before we eat."

She opened the car door as soon as he stopped. "I'll be back soon. I have everything packed."

Vicky carried a small basket when she returned and Chad opened the trunk to store it. When Vicky sat beside him, she placed a box on the seat between them.

"I made some cookies. We can snack on them if we get hungry."

As he pulled away from the curb, Chad asked, "Do you like to cook?"

"I cooked when I was at home, but I don't do much for myself. I usually just prepare food a couple of times a week and live on leftovers the rest of the time."

"Where to?"

"Go south until we come to I-270, drive on it until we come to Route 33 and head southeast. I'll direct you when we need to leave that road to reach the park."

"I know very little about Ohio. Tell me about this park while we're driving."

"I'm a native Ohioan, so I'll admit I'm prejudiced, but I think our state has more diversity than most states in the union. We have Lake Erie to the north, several large cities, and the Ohio River and its industrial sites to the southwest. You saw part of our vast farming area when we took our drive east of Columbus, and there's a lot more west of Columbus."

"I sure enjoyed seeing the farming region on Thursday."

She accepted his comment with a smile. "But of all our scenic attractions, I think I'm partial to what we're going to see today. Mom and Dad did a lot of camping in this area when I was a kid. At first Dad just pitched a tent at one of the campgrounds and we roughed it, and I remember those vacations more than the times we rented a cabin." Her mouth curved into a steady smile of happiness. "It was the highlight of our summer."

Chad slowed almost to a crawl, for an oversize loaded truck was in front of him, and he glanced at Vicky, analyzing a subtle change in her voice that he hadn't heard before when she spoke of her parents.

"You must have had a wonderful childhood."

Vicky had been staring straight ahead, seemingly lost in happy memories, but she quickly transferred her gaze to him.

"Yes, of course. We were a happy threesome until I disappointed my folks by dropping out of college. They had dreams for me, you see, and I couldn't live up to them. It's not their fault that our relationships are strained—it's me."

Not willing to probe until Vicky was ready to confide in him, Chad passed the slow-moving vehicle and the moment passed.

"The hills are made of sandstone, a composition that lends itself to the formation of caves. There are several recess caves where Native Americans lived long before Europeans came to North America. Hiking trails cover the majority of the forested area and take the hiker along towering cliffs, waterfalls and deep gorges. Someday you should come to some of the programs held at the park and hear geologists talk about the formation of Hocking Hills."

They were both hungry by the time they entered the park and Vicky directed Chad to follow the signs to Old Man's Cave. The parking lot wasn't crowded and he parked close to the trail that accessed the picnic area. Sun filtered through the barren tree trunks and a mild breeze brought a hint of decaying leaves.

"Not a bad day for the first week of November."

"I suppose I should apologize for not carrying the picnic basket," Chad said when Vicky opened the trunk of her car to get the food. "The thermos doesn't look like it will be too heavy for me, so I'll carry that. People will think I'm as strong as a horse, so just pretend you don't know me if people look at us, perhaps wondering why a big hulk like me would let *you* carry the heaviest load."

Vicky felt warm and enchanted by his mild humor.

"It isn't a big basket, so no problem. Let's look for a place in the shade. It's always cool in this glade, but the temperatures are supposed to rise to the eighties today."

"We'd better enjoy the mild weather. I'm sure we won't have many more autumn days like this. You lead the way."

Following Vicky toward a table, Chad tried to identify the trees—many that he hadn't known in his home state of Alabama. Vicky glanced over her shoulder to see if he was all right and he gave her a smile that sent her pulse racing. His eyes were alive with affection and delight. Their eyes held for a timeless moment until Vicky stumbled. Her near-fall brought her thoughts back to earth and she walked on, wondering just how much their shared moment meant to Chad. When the trail widened, she slowed her steps until he was at her side.

"You're looking wonderful today."

"I'm feeling great. At my last appointment with the surgeon, he said I was doing so well that I wouldn't have to see him for another month unless there were complications. The first thing I thought of when I got up this morning was that it's been six weeks today. That day I got up feeling on top of the world—the adrenaline was really pumping like always on game day." His voice faded away and Vicky prayed silently for wisdom to know how to deal with him today.

Two other families occupied the picnic area and Vicky headed toward an isolated table shaded by a gold-tinged maple tree. Silently, Chad helped her spread a cloth on the table. She didn't want to chatter but she had to say something to lighten his mood.

"I'm not the best cook in the world so don't expect gourmet food. When I get really hungry, I drop by my parents' house for a good meal." She put a plastic bowl and foil-wrapped sandwiches on the table. "How does fresh fruit and melon with ham salad sandwiches sound to you?"

"Like a banquet," he said, and Vicky was heartened that he spoke cheerily, in spite of the sadness reflected in his dark eyes. He poured iced tea into the cups she placed in the center of the table. "Mom insisted that I learn how to cook, and I did help around the kitchen. I lived at home during my college years, but after I started playing with the NFL, I ate out most of the time."

Chad waited until she was seated before he carefully lowered his body to the low bench. When she started to unwrap the sandwiches, he said, "I'd like to say grace if it's okay."

She nodded, and he reached across the table and took her hand that hovered over the sandwiches.

"Lord," he said confidently as a man would who was accustomed to praying often, "I have so much to thank You for that I'm ashamed of hanging on to the past. Forgive me and give me the courage to get through this difficult experience and anticipate a new life. Thank you for sending Vicky to encourage me and for allowing us to share this experience. Thanks for the food she's prepared and work Your will in her life, too. Amen."

His voice faded to a hushed stillness and Vicky felt the sting of tears behind her eyelids. She longed to encourage him, and she prayed for wisdom to be the kind of friend he needed. With their hands still clasped, she said, "Remember, we're in this together. I've enjoyed every minute of our time together."

He lifted her hand to his lips, and the kiss he placed on her palm was as soft as a whisper. When his gaze rested on hers, Vicky felt a gentle affection coming from him, and her heart turned over in response.

"So have I, Vicky. I've thought from the first that God brought us together for a purpose, and the more I'm with you, I've started wondering if He has more in store for us than a brief friendship."

Flustered by what he seemed to be suggesting and not knowing how to answer, she placed a sandwich on his plate and took the lid off the plastic bowl that held the fruit mixture.

"Have you made any more headway on sorting your mail?"

"Not much. So much of it calls for decisions I'm not ready to make yet. I gave my agent strict orders not to contact me, but he has forwarded a lot of offers that I suppose I'll have to deal with."

"I don't suppose there's any rush about any of it."

He shook his head indecisively. "I'm not so sure. I'll tell you what some of them are, if you don't mind being bored with my affairs."

"Not at all. I can't help you make decisions, but I can listen."

"A national TV network wants to produce

a commentary about my life. Howie thinks he can sell a biography of my life. After only a few years of playing pro ball, I'm not sure I'm that popular. However, he's talked to one publisher who's interested. I have had an outstanding record since I started playing in high school. The editor thinks he can publish my life as an inspirational book, highlighting my rise to fame, the sudden end of my career and how my faith in God carried me through the drastic changes in my life."

"That sounds interesting. Is there any hurry in making your decision?"

"Yes, I think so. I'm big news now, but within a year when I'm no longer in the national spotlight, Chad Reece will just be another has-been. And public attention will turn to new heroes. I can see the necessity of moving quickly."

"Then why are you hesitating?"

"I'm not sure. I suppose I'm still smarting over my illegitimate birth, and if people start poking around in my past, that's bound to come out."

"I don't see why that would be embarrassing after all these years—you can't be blamed for what your parents did."

"I wasn't considering myself. I came to terms a long time ago with that fact that my mother probably wasn't married when I was born. I'm still angry at my parents for not telling me who I was, but I'm not so angry that I want to embarrass Perry and Lorene. He's highly regarded in the academic world—I don't want to be the one to reveal his past."

He paused thoughtfully and Vicky respected his silence. She watched a squirrel scurrying across the ground. Several blue jays perched near a feeder filled with sunflower seeds kept up a steady racket of harsh calls as they snatched full beaks of food.

Several minutes passed before Chad said, "If I write the book, I suppose I could be selective in what goes into print. I don't have anything else to do now."

"Have you done much writing?"

A crooked grin answered her. "No. I wouldn't have a clue how to write a book. I agonized over my term papers in college. Probably I should gather the information about my life and let the publishers furnish a ghostwriter. That's what they've suggested."

"That sounds like the only solution," she agreed enthusiastically. "It would provide the emotional release you need now. It could serve as a sort of transition between where you are now, where you've been, and where you're going."

"That's how I see it. But I want to make the right decision. Will you pray for me?"

"Of course!" She didn't intend to offer much advice because only Chad could deal effectively with the change in his lifestyle. But she silently thanked God that he seemed to be accepting his new life.

They had eaten all of the sandwiches and the fruit, so Vicky stood, gathered up the plates and wrappings and put them in the garbage can. "Do you feel up to hiking?"

"I'd like to take the trail up that little hill. I've walked a lot but haven't done any climbing. I think I'm ready for it."

"It's a gradual climb through the forest. You'll have no trouble as long as we walk slowly. I'll take the basket to the car and be right back."

Chad watched her long, graceful stride as she walked with ease toward the parking lot. God had been gracious when He'd sent Vicky to help him. Unlike the women he had encountered during his NFL career, she didn't seem to expect anything from him. He considered himself a shrewd judge of character, and he wondered if Vicky's only interest in him was to help him overcome the difficult situation that had come his way. Considering the things they had shared, would the day come when they could walk away from one another and forget their time together? He didn't believe that would happen. Some tangible bond was forming between them. Could it be love? Although he'd had his share of puppy love romances and had even dated occasionally in high school, Chad had been too wrapped up in his career to give any serious thought to love, home and a family. But over the past weeks, when he thought of the future, he realized that he didn't want to live alone, and if he did share his life with someone, he thought Vicky would be his choice.

They walked single file along the narrow trail that zigzagged frequently to moderate the steep ascent. It didn't prove difficult for Vicky, apparently, because she climbed effortlessly. Chad sensed that she was tempering her gait so he wouldn't have to walk fast to keep up with her.

When they came to a wooden bench beside the trail, Vicky sat down. "Ready for a rest?"

"More than ready. I'd been doing so well walking along the streets of Columbus that I thought I was back in shape. I guess I've not recovered as much as I thought." He drew a steadying breath as he dropped down on the bench at her side.

"You look tired today," Vicky said. "Are you sure you aren't doing too much?"

He shook his head. "Not doing—worrying too much."

She looked at him, questioning, waiting for him to explain.

"The preacher's message hit me dead center," he said. "I'm ashamed to admit it, but I feel pretty small when I compare my attitude to Job's."

"Everyone has lapses of faith. I struggle with it all the time."

"I suppose that's the reason you understand my shortcomings."

"As I've told you before—my problems don't seem like much when I compare them to yours. I think you're allowed to lapse into self-pity sometimes. If I'd suffered the reverses you have, I'd be bawling my eyes out."

"It irritates me that I'm dwelling on the things I've lost rather than the things I still have. I wish I could just trust the future to God." He sighed with frustration.

"What other choice do you have? There's no other way to deal with the future."

"I admit my thoughts aren't too coherent. I guess I've had things going my way for too long. But I can't dwell on gloomy thoughts in this beautiful area. Let's walk a little farther.

The more I see of this place, the more I think I'd like to spend a few weeks here."

"The park offers plenty of camping opportunities. You can rough it and live in a tent like we did or stay in a cabin. Or even better, if you still want to avoid people, you could rent an RV and park at one of the campsites. Everything you need would be in the camper."

"I like that idea," he agreed. "I'll think about it. And now, if you don't mind, I'm ready to go back to Columbus. I know my limit and I've about reached it."

"If you decide to go that route, you'll find several rental agencies in the phone book."

The light was blinking on Vicky's answering machine when she entered the apartment. She punched the button.

"Vicky, this is Mom. Give me a call when you get home."

Vicky had anticipated reliving the euphoric day she had spent with Chad and she didn't want to return the call. But if she didn't her mother would probably think the worst and send out a dragnet for her. She dialed her parents' number.

"Hi, Mom. Did you need to talk to me?"

"I called two or three times today. Did you just get home?"

"Mom! I'm an adult now—I don't need a keeper."

"I'm not so sure about that. That is, if you've been out all day with Chad Reece."

Seething with frustration, Vicky didn't answer.

"You know I don't like to interfere in your life."

"Then don't do it! I left home to prove to you that I can take care of myself."

"I can't stand by and let you get involved with Chad like you did with Damon. I thought that experience would have taught you something."

Tears stung Vicky's eyelids and she wanted to hang up on her mother. The day with Chad had left her feeling serene and healed—as if by sharing his recovery, she could put her past mistakes behind her and face a new life. How could she make her mother understand?

"Chad has had a bad experience and I want to help him through this crisis. His whole life has been ruined and he needs someone to talk to."

"And as soon as he's well, he'll move out of your life just like Damon did."

"I expect him to. My relationship with Chad doesn't compare to what happened with Damon."

Rachel continued as if Vicky hadn't spoken, and every word brought a searing pain to her heart. "Face it, Vicky. You don't show any wisdom when it comes to men. Even as a child, you made poor choices in your friends. Remember the time you took a migrant farmer's child under your wing at school. She could speak only a few words of English, but you were determined to help. You were devastated when her parents moved on."

Vicky closed her eyes and collapsed into the nearest chair. Despair swept over her as her mother continued to cite instances when Vicky's efforts to help others had brought sorrow to her. Rachel had never seemed to realize that her critical assessments of Vicky's friendships had added salt to her festering wounds when she lost those friends.

"Are you listening to me? I'm only telling you these things because I don't want to see you get hurt again."

Vicky's hands trembled, and her throat was so tight that she didn't know if she could speak. With an effort, she said, "I'm listening, but not for long. Goodbye."

She severed the connection and laid the receiver on the table. She knew her mother would try to call again, and Vicky *could not* talk to her now. She had never talked back to her mother and she knew that in her present state of mind she would say things that she would regret always. She stood and paced around the apartment, as she seethed with anger and humiliation.

Did her mother think she enjoyed the raw sores of an aching heart? She had gone through that twice already, and she believed her heart was seared to prevent her falling in love ever again. It was obvious to her that Chad wanted only her friendship and she was content with that.

Exhausted from the afternoon of physical exercise and her mother's censure, Vicky's self-confidence plummeted as she recalled the callous way Damon had abandoned her. A heaviness centered in her chest when she acknowledged that her mother's assessment was right. She *didn't* have any common sense when it came to romantic relationships. After Chad left, she would avoid male companionship. It was safer that way.

Vicky changed into her nightgown and took up her Bible. A hot tear rolled down her cheek, and then another and another until the tears dripped on the pages of the Bible. She tried to bite back the tears, but when she couldn't, she laid the Bible aside and got into bed. Her mother had opened an old wound, and although she knew that crying didn't solve anything, the tears continued to flow until she slept from sheer exhaustion.

Chapter Seven

After a night's rest, Vicky's suggestions about going camping still sounded good and Chad borrowed Grace's phone book. After two calls he found what he needed. He contacted the taxi driver who had volunteered to chauffeur him and had the cabbie take him to the rental agency. After resisting the high-pressure salesman's pitch, he chose a modest five-year-old motor home, which provided everything he would need. He didn't want to call attention to himself by traveling in a pretentious RV. He paid an advance on the cost of the vehicle for two weeks.

He didn't intend for anyone except Vicky to know where he was. He would take the cell phone so he could communicate with her. He wasn't so lacking in consideration that he wouldn't let his parents know what he was doing, however, so after he returned to his apartment he telephoned them.

Mrs. Reece answered the phone when he called.

"Hi, Mom."

"Oh, Chad," she said, "I'm so relieved to hear from you. How are you getting along?"

"Just great. I'm going camping for a couple of weeks."

"Camping! Are you able to do that?"

"Yes, and I'm looking forward to it. I haven't been camping since church camp when I was a boy."

"Where are you going?" she asked.

"I'm still hiding, Mom, so it's better if I don't tell you where I'll be. I may call you, but don't worry if I don't."

"It will be impossible not to worry," she said. "I wish you'd come home, Chad."

"Maybe at Christmas, but not before."

When his father came to the phone, he asked, "Have you talked to Perry or Lorene? They've called here several times to see about you. They deserve better treatment, Chad. You also have a sister now. This isn't like you."

Chad didn't take offense at his father's tone, because he knew he deserved the reprimand. "I'm not like I used to be in many ways, Dad, but I'll give them a call."

The happiness in Lorene's voice when she heard his voice a few minutes later seared Chad's conscience. "Perry," she called, "it's Chad. Pick up the other phone."

"How are things?" Perry said in his deep, pleasant voice.

"Physically, I'm in great condition. The surgeon checked me out last week, and he's pleased with my recovery. How are *you*?"

"Very well. But my doctor wants me to come to Columbus in three months and let the surgeon look me over."

"I'll come, too," Lorene said eagerly. "If you're still there, we can see you."

"I think I will be, but I'm not making any long-term plans at the moment." He explained about his planned retreat. "When I finish that, I hope I'll have my head sorted out, so I'll know what to do. Right now, I'm totally confused."

"I wish you had someone in Columbus to help you," Lorene said. "You've cut everyone off, but you do need someone to talk to."

"As a matter of fact, I have someone," he said. "I don't know if you even saw her, but Vicky Lanham, a volunteer, sat with me several nights when I was in the hospital to give Mom and Dad a break. We've kept in touch and have become good friends. She pointed me in the right direction for a nice apartment, and I went to church with her last Sunday. She's the only one who knows where I'll be for several days."

"That relieves my mind considerably," Lorene said. "I can understand your need to be alone—I suppose you got that from me. When I'm troubled, I'm better off alone than in a crowd."

"When I was a kid, I sometimes noticed things about me that were different from my parents. I wondered then if I'd gotten that trait from a parent or grandparent I'd never seen. So now I know."

"We aren't going to force ourselves on you," Perry assured him. "We're here like we've always been. We'll accept whatever part of your life you want us to have."

"I hope to spend these next few days considering my future. When I get back to Columbus, I hope I'll have my life sorted out."

"Don't expect a blueprint of your future," Lorene said. "I learned the hard way that I had to take a day at a time on faith."

"Yeah… 'The just shall live by faith.' God gave me that message a few days ago. It isn't easy to accept. Anyways, I'll be in touch."

"God bless you, Chad," Perry said before he hung up.

* * *

Looking in the mirror on the day Chad picked up the rental camper and headed for Hocking Hills State Park, he saw a face that could have been a stranger's staring back at him. He didn't think anyone would suspect who he was. From head to toe, he looked more like a lumberjack than a pro football player.

He wore brown waterproof vulcanized rubber boots with a specially engineered sole for climbing mountains or walking on snow and ice. His trousers were made of heavy corduroy. Over his T-shirt, he wore a chili-red flannel shirt. A weatherproof cap with lined earflaps was perched on his black hair. Over his arm he carried a hooded reversible parka. Chad had thought of growing a beard to conceal his identity, but only his closest friends would recognize him in this getup.

He hadn't owned any outdoor gear, and he didn't want to stick out like a sore thumb in brand-new clothes, so he went to a store that carried used garments and bought everything he needed. In a store catering to hunters he'd purchased a backpack, a hiker's medical kit and a thermos.

Vicky agreed to let him rent the camper in her name for two weeks, so he wouldn't be leaving a paper trail behind him. She took him to pick up the RV, and he squeezed her hand when they parted at the parking lot. "Thanks for all your help. I'm hoping to find my way before I see you again."

"You will if you don't want to look too far into the future," she said. "If you keep that up, you'll be miserable. God expects us to trust Him. Personally, I'd just as soon the future is obscure."

Now that it was time for him to cut loose his moorings, Chad realized that he hated to leave Vicky behind. Over the past weeks, she'd been like the Rock of Gibraltar to him firm, unwavering, always there. Momentarily, he wished she could go with him, but that would defeat the purpose he'd set up for himself. Besides, it was out of the question for them to camp together.

"You still haven't told me why you're disillusioned. I apologize for being so selfish—thinking of myself, not of you," Chad said.

She waved away his apology. "Remember," Vicky said, as he started the engine. "I won't call you, but you can call anytime you want to talk."

As he carefully steered the RV out of Columbus and accessed Route 33, Chad felt as if he was leaving his old self behind. When he returned would he feel like a new man—one beginning again?

As she stood beside her car and watched Chad slowly maneuver the camper out of the parking lot, Vicky welcomed a few days without his company. While she had sympathized with and encouraged Chad to look on the brighter side, she often remembered the proverb Jesus once quoted in relation to His ministry.

"Physician, heal yourself."

She'd given plenty of advice to Chad, and if she continued in this mission she thought God was calling her to do, it was time for her to deal with her own rebellion.

Was it time to stop focusing on Chad and think about her own future? She readily admitted that she was wasting her life. The hours she spent at the bookstore had turned into drudgery, and she was determined to find some answer to her own problems.

When she wasn't working, she spent hours driving along the rural roads around Columbus, carefully avoiding byways that would take her close to Hocking Hills State Park. She didn't want to be tempted to drop in on Chad. He had to make the first move if he wanted to see her.

As she drove she kept hearing over and over

in her subconscious, "Return to Bethel." She associated these words with Jacob, one of the Israelite patriarchs in the Old Testament, later to be known as Israel. Finally, one evening, she looked up the story in the Bible.

Jacob had run away from home to escape the wrath of his brother, Esau. During his flight, God appeared to Jacob in a vision. God assured Jacob that He would be with him during his exile in a foreign land, making it plain that his exile was only temporary. God would eventually bring Jacob back to the land he was to inherit, where his descendants would become as plentiful as the dust of the earth. God's revelation to Jacob contained the promise that *all* people would be blessed through Jacob and his descendants.

"God, thank You," she prayed, "that I was included in that 'all' when I repented of my sins and accepted Jesus as my Savior. Once I made a promise to You that I would carry Your message to people who had never heard of You or Your Son. I've failed You, Father—forgive me. Give me another chance."

Jacob had believed God's promise and he had vowed,

"If God will be with me and will watch over me on this journey I am taking and will give me food to eat and clothes to wear so that I return safely to my father's house, then the Lord will be my God."

Jacob spent years in a foreign land, but the promise could not be fulfilled until Jacob returned to Bethel to accept the mission that God had chosen for him. Vicky couldn't get her mind off the promise she had made. She had spent three troubled years because she had forsaken her vow. She was also distressed because she had allowed a rift to widen with her parents. Jacob had to reconcile with his brother and father before he could receive the promise.

Was God telling her to renew the vow she had made years ago? Would she be able to do that without asking her parents' forgiveness for ignoring their advice and going her own way?

Vicky knew what she had to do, but as she shrugged out of her terry robe and crawled between the covers of the bed, she wondered if she had the courage to do it. How had Jacob felt when he had to admit to his brother that he had wronged him? She snapped off the bedside lamp and lay a long time in the darkness. She prayed for sleep but lay awake most of the night.

The next morning, Vicky stood beneath the warm water of the shower nozzle, languid and uncertain about the decision she had made. She wrapped herself in a large towel and stood where she could look at the television in the living room as she fashioned her hair.

"Cold and breezy today. Kiss goodbye to our beautiful fall weather," the meteorologist reported gleefully, as if he welcomed the end of autumn.

"Not me," Vicky said, shivering. The owner of the apartment hadn't turned on the central heat yet, and her small space heater didn't do much to warm the apartment. Her thoughts strayed to Chad. She would like to know what he was doing.

Vicky unzipped a garment bag that held her winter clothing and picked out a pair of fleece pants and a top with a lined mandarin collar. Brown leather boots completed her outfit. She bundled into a hip-length lined fleece jacket. In spite of the cold wind, she decided to walk to work. As she walked she contemplated how she could implement her need to "Return to Bethel."

Now that she knew God wasn't finished with her, Vicky felt as if the weight she had carried for so long had been lifted from her shoulders. She prayed that Chad was also finding peace in his heart.

Even the small bookstore, which had seemed

like a prison to her, was more inviting today now that her mind was at rest. She felt more energetic than she had in months, and her hands needed something to do. She washed the display window and chose several books dealing with Thanksgiving. She searched the internet and found pictures depicting the coming of the Pilgrims to the New World. She downloaded the pictures and shaped them into a large collage. Her employer was impressed, and Vicky herself was pleased with the outcome. She'd been fretting for months over her lack of witnessing when she could have been spreading the Good News at the bookstore. Why had it taken her this long to realize that involvement in mission work always started at home?

Vicky hadn't expected to hear from Chad for several days, if at all, while he was gone. But the phone rang the next morning while she was putting away her summer clothes and getting winter things out of the storage bags. Chad's smooth voice filled her ears.

"Just reporting in. I thought you might want to know that the camper and I made it to the park without incident."

"I wondered if you were settled in."

"Yes. I'm in a campground close to Old Man's Cave, which I intend to explore today.

I fixed my own breakfast in the camper, but there's a small restaurant close by if I want to eat out."

"Is the campground crowded?"

"About half of the campsites are occupied. But I don't have anyone close. Oh, I guess I'll have to revise that—a large motor home is pulling in right beside me. So I guess I'll have company whether I want it or not."

"Have you done any hiking?"

"On some of the short trails. I'm going on a longer hike today, gradually working up my strength until I can walk from Old Man's Cave to Cedar Falls to Ash Cave in one day. That's six miles, I think. I may rent a bedroll and spend a night or two outdoors."

"According to the meteorologist, we're going to have several days of cold weather."

"I haven't bothered to listen to any news, although there is a small TV in the camper if I take a notion to turn it on. If it's too cold I won't sleep out at night. I feel as if I'm physically recovered, but the surgeon suggested that I should watch out for colds and viruses. When do you have a day off?"

"Friday."

"Want to come and visit me?"

"That would be nice. Thanks for the invitation. I'll wear my hiking clothes. It's been a while since I've walked in the forest."

He gave her directions to his campsite. Chad had always been a "people" person, so it didn't surprise him that he had soon grown tired of his self-imposed isolation. When he was still physically recovering from his surgery, it had been easy to avoid people. It felt good to want to see people again.

Although he looked forward to seeing Vicky, he wasn't sure he wanted a camper as close as the one that had just pulled in. With all the empty places to choose, why would the owner park right beside his RV?

The Fifth Wheel camper was pulled by a pickup truck—neither of them very new. The driver parked, stepped out of the truck and stretched as if he'd been traveling a long distance. Chad turned from the window to prepare his breakfast.

He poured cold cereal into a bowl, added milk and toasted a slice of brown bread and spread it with margarine. He turned on the television and watched the local news as he ate. After he rinsed the few utensils he'd used and placed them on a rack to dry, he looked out the window and saw his neighbor still puttering around the motor home.

Chad stepped out on the steps and called, "Need any help?"

The man, probably in his sixties, flashed a smile and walked toward Chad.

"I never turn down help when it's offered. But I don't have anything to do now, unless you'll come in for some breakfast and talk to me a spell. I get lonesome traveling alone." He stuck out his right hand. "My name's Oliver."

Chad squeezed his hand. "Glad to meet you. I'm Chad."

Since Oliver hadn't given a last name, he didn't think it was necessary to mention his. He wanted to stay incognito if at all possible.

"I've already had my breakfast, but I'll take a cup of tea with you, if you have some handy."

Chad closed the few feet between their trailers and bent his head to clear the low door as he followed Oliver inside.

"I don't have anything but decaf."

"That's fine."

Oliver motioned Chad to a chair at the small table beside a window. While Oliver ran water into a kettle, put a skillet on the stove, opened a can of frozen biscuits and put them in the oven, Chad looked over his host and his living quarters.

Oliver was a slender man—one who would never stand out in a crowd. Small-boned and of medium height, his movements were swift and competent as he moved around the small space. Chad studied his face. He had a kindly mouth and his compassionate olive-green eyes brimmed with a compelling, indefinable emotion. Long, thin hair hung over his forehead. He was dressed in faded jeans and a turtleneck sweater that had seen better days.

When he broke two eggs into the sizzling oil in the skillet, the aroma tempted Chad, and he said, "How about frying another one of those for me? That smell makes me think I'm back home in Mom's kitchen again."

"Where is home?"

"Alabama, but I've been away from there a long time." Unwilling to talk about his past, even to a stranger, Chad continued, "Where's your home?"

Amusement flickered in Oliver's eyes. "You're sitting in it."

Chad's expression must have registered his astonishment and concern, for Oliver's eyes crinkled in merriment. "I'm kind of a vagabond, and it's not a bad way to live. Over the past few years I've been in every state in the Union and have met lots of interesting people."

"But how do you decide where to go?"

"If it's left up to me, I go south in the winter and north in the summer. But I leave it up to the Good Lord to guide me and lots of times He directs me to places I've never heard of. And would just as soon not go," he added with a humorous glint in his eyes.

Chad decided he was talking too much. He wasn't in a position to give answers about his life, so he shouldn't be asking questions of others.

Oliver set a plate before Chad. It had two eggs, instead of the one he'd asked for, turned over but the yolks still quivery enough to suit Chad. Two golden-brown biscuits were also on the plate. Oliver put margarine and jelly within Chad's reach. Sitting on the opposite side of the table, Oliver bowed his head.

"For Your gracious bounty, we thank You, Lord. Bless my new friend, Chad, and bring peace to his heart. Amen."

Momentarily Chad wondered how Oliver knew he needed peace in his heart, but he turned his attention to the food that tasted better than anything he'd eaten since his accident. They ate mostly in silence, and when he finished, Chad thanked Oliver for the food and excused himself.

"I'm going hiking this morning. Are you acquainted with the forest? If not, I can give you some information about the trails."

"This is my first trip to this forest, and I want to look it over."

"You can hike with me if you want to."

Chad surprised himself with the invitation. He'd come to the forest for solitude, hadn't he? And already he'd invited Vicky *and* Oliver to walk with him. Still, he was pleased when Oliver agreed to go along if Chad would wait until he could get ready.

The next two days they covered many miles of the forest, and Oliver seemed tireless. In fact, the older man's stamina exceeded Chad's own. Oliver never asked any questions, nor did Chad, and most of their hiking was done in silence.

Chad called Vicky on Thursday night and asked her to stop in Logan and pick up pizza for their lunch. He mentioned his companionship with Oliver and asked if it was all right if he hiked with them. Still smarting from the heated conversation with her mother, Vicky hesitated to be alone with Chad after her mother's assessment of their relationship. She readily agreed to his suggestion that they ask Oliver to share their pizza and accompany them as they walked.

The next day when they crowded around the table in Chad's small camper to eat the pizza and chocolate cake Vicky had brought, Chad said, "I've been here over a week, and I still haven't learned why part of the park is called Old Man's Cave."

"Oh, I can tell you that," Vicky said. "Before Ohio was settled, a hermit by the name of Richard Rowe took up lodging in the cave. He and his dogs didn't do much except hunt as far as I know, but he lived out his life in this area and is buried under the ledge of the cave."

"After roaming these woods for a week," Chad said, "I can understand why people wanted to settle here. It isn't any surprise to me that this is your favorite part of Ohio. It was lucky for me that you remembered it so well and steered me in this direction."

When they were finished, Vicky helped Chad wash the few dishes. "Where are we going to hike today? I want to leave in time to get home before too late."

"How about to Cedar Falls and back?" Chad asked.

"That works for me."

"We'll plan to get back in time to have a meal at the lodge before you have to leave for Columbus," Chad assured her when they set out on their hike.

With an overabundance of fathers already, during the week he spent daily in Oliver's presence, Chad realized that he had adopted a filial attitude toward the older man. But at the end of a week, they knew little more about each other than they had at the beginning.

Chad had finally decided that he was strong enough to hike from Old Man's Cave to Ash Cave and back again. When the meteorologist promised mild weather, Chad suggested the long hike and Oliver agreed. They put food and plenty of water in backpacks and set out about ten o'clock, with Chad leading the way and setting the pace as usual.

They stopped in the shelter of a rocky projection overlooking a gorge to have their lunch. They were protected from the keen wind that spoke of winter, but the sun's beacon filtered through the barren tree limbs and warmed the place where they sat. Oliver had talked very little about his faith, yet Chad had sensed that his new friend had a close and abiding walk with God. He felt compelled to talk to Oliver about his situation.

After he ate a sandwich, Chad took a banana from his backpack, and as he ate the fruit, he glanced at Oliver, who sat with his eyes closed enjoying the warmth of the sun's rays on his upturned face.

"Do you know who I am?" Chad asked.

Oliver opened his eyes slightly and squinted

at Chad. "No more than you've told me. Should I know you?"

"I thought you might. Are you a football fan?"

Oliver shook his head. "Nope. Never could understand the game. I'm partial to baseball, but I watch some basketball, too."

He slid across the rock ledge and leaned against the trunk of a sturdy oak growing precipitously close to the edge of the cliff. "I've wondered about you a lot. It's plain you're a healthy, well-educated man and I can't figure why you're wandering around this forest as if you don't have any responsibilities. Most men of your caliber would be working at an important job, probably married and with a family. You have been a mystery to me. Who are you and why *are* you here?"

"Trying to find a purpose for my aimless life."

He couldn't keep the dejection and bitterness out of his voice, and Oliver cast a speculative glance in his direction. Chad stared into the deep gorge below them and took a slow breath. This was the first time he'd talked about his injury and shattered dreams to someone who didn't know anything about it.

"I started playing football when I was twelve. I loved the sport and from day one my goal was to play on a professional team. I continued playing during my college years. When I was drafted and later hired to play for the NFL, my heart was full and overflowing with thanksgiving to God for helping me achieve what I had always wanted. The first two years were like a dream come true to me. That changed two months ago. Instead of a dream my life turned into a nightmare."

Chad's throat ached, and the pain in his heart that he thought had eased, surfaced and gnawed at the fragile thread of optimism he had for his future. The anguish consuming him wouldn't let him sit quietly. He jumped to his feet, wrapped his arm around a slender tree that leaned toward the gorge. How simple it would be to let go and fall—that would end the torment of his soul. Not trusting himself, he jumped away from the tree and back into the safety of the rocky overhang of the cliff.

Desperation in his voice, Chad continued, "During the first game of this season, I received a serious injury. In short—I can't play football again. My future is ruined."

Chad sensed the compassion in Oliver's heart when he softly said, "I'm sorry. I know how it hurts to lose a dream."

Briefly Chad sketched the rest of the story. How the accident happened. The startling discovery of his birth. His anger at both sets of parents. The circumstances leading to his friendship with Vicky. His faltering faith.

His uncertain future.

Oliver listened in silence until Chad, spent by his anguished revelation, slid to the ground exhausted. Not a sound could be heard in the forest except the faint rustling of wind stirring the branches of a pine tree clinging to the stony cliff above them.

"If you're a child of God," Oliver said softly, "and I believe you are, *there is no uncertain future*. Life on earth might be uncertain, but eternity in Heaven is a sure thing. Now I think you should hear my story, which isn't a pleasant one, either."

"I've hesitated to pry into your affairs, but I'll admit I've wondered about you, too," Chad said with a wan smile.

Oliver's countenance was serene, as if he had told this story so many times that it no longer held any anguish for him.

"When I was in my teens, I received a call from God to preach the Gospel. I didn't doubt that the call was sincere. But I went into the army, served four years, fell in love with a servicewoman and married her. We had two children, and although on occasion I remembered the time God laid His hand on my life, I was too busy making a living to answer that call. Ten years ago, I was a successful contractor. Preaching the Word was the furthest thing from my mind."

Oliver's anguished expression tore at Chad's heart. Oliver shuddered, and Chad reached out his hand, hoping to comfort his friend. But Oliver had closed his eyes and didn't see Chad's gesture. He had shoved his hands into his pockets and leaned forward, weaving back and forth as he talked.

"This is too difficult for you," Chad said. "I don't need to hear."

Chad couldn't control his gasp of surprise when Oliver said, "But you're meant to hear it. You *must* listen. God sent me here to tell you my story."

Chapter Eight

After a long pause, Oliver continued, "I didn't heed God's call to preach until a tragedy came into my life four years ago. I learned that God didn't expect me to preach from a pulpit like most of his servants. I'm an itinerant evangelist. When I start out on a trip, I never know where I'm going. I follow God's leading, and God always directs me to a place where someone needs me."

Chad stared at Oliver in astonishment, and hair rose at the nape of his neck when he comprehended the significance of what he was hearing. Had Moses felt this way when God appeared to him and Moses was told he was "standing on holy ground"?

"I was in Indiana six weeks ago intending to go to Arizona for the winter. When I got to I-70, I turned east instead of west. Now, understand I don't have a pillar of fire at night or a cloud by day to guide me like God guided the Hebrews, but God speaks to my heart and gives me directions. I never know when God is going to tell me to 'fold my tents' and move on, either. Do you find that hard to believe?"

"No, sir," Chad whispered.

"Of all the places I could have put my motor home I was prompted to park beside yours. I didn't know why God wanted me to speak to you or what He wanted me to say, but I knew immediately that I was to minister to you."

"Then you believe God brought us together for a reason."

"Yes, I believe that. Don't you?"

Chad nodded his head slowly. "Yes, I do. But I don't know how your situation compares to mine."

"Then let me go back a few years. I had an accident, too. I was traveling with my family along a narrow road in Pennsylvania. An 18-wheeler rear-ended my van and shoved it into the path of an oncoming pickup. My wife and two daughters were killed in the impact and I was in the hospital and rehab for months."

Oliver paused when two hikers approached. Chad answered their greeting and waited for Oliver to continue.

"I had so many broken bones the surgeons

didn't think I would ever walk again. After the death of my family, I didn't have any close relatives and I knew no one in the little town where I was hospitalized, because our home was in New York. But the pastor and congregation of a local church sort of adopted me. They visited me, prayed for me, and I gradually healed both physically and emotionally. When I left the medical facility they provided a small cottage for me to live in."

Oliver paused to catch his breath and took a handkerchief out of his pocket and wiped his eyes.

"Sounds almost like the story of the prophet Elisha and how God sent someone to provide for him," Chad said.

"My insurance didn't cover my expenses," Oliver went on, "and with the added cost of a triple funeral and burial, which I couldn't even attend, I was bankrupt. All I had left was enough to buy the truck and motor home I have now."

Momentarily Chad wondered if God had sent Oliver to him so he could buy some new traveling equipment for him.

"During those months when I was flat on my back, God finally got my attention. I remembered the time He'd laid His hand on me and I'd refused His call."

"And you never blamed God for allowing your family to be destroyed like that?"

"Ah, Chad, God didn't send the accident that took my family. It was caused by the recklessness of a man. It's part of human life to suffer trouble. God has never promised that His followers will go through life without adversity. I wish I could tell you that I felt that way all along. But I have to admit that I was a broken man for months, and my thoughts about God were bitter and spiteful. Why had He let my family die?"

Chad had been holding back his tears, but the sorrow in Oliver's voice, which reminded him of his own doubts, caused tears to run down his cheeks. *God, give me the words to comfort him.*

"I gradually got over my anger," Oliver continued slowly, "when I remembered that God had lost a Son—a beloved Son that He had sent to be a Sacrifice for the sins of the whole world. If mankind hadn't sinned in the first place, there wouldn't have been sorrow in the world. But God made humans with a free will—and too often we have made wrong choices. I did."

Oliver paused and Chad listened to the sighing of the pines around them. He sensed that God's presence had infiltrated this lonely spot making it a cathedral. He lifted his hands in worship as he listened to the rest of Oliver's story.

"I've never been able to read the mind of God—to know why He set me aside for a certain task, but He did. I've been following this ministry for a few years now and God has blessed me in many ways."

"But how do you live? It takes money for gas, upkeep on your vehicles."

Oliver stood and buckled on his backpack as they prepared to continue their hike.

"God provides. Sometimes I stay in an area for several months, and I pick up some carpentry work, using the skills of my old contracting job. Also, after I'd been in this ministry for a while, I had an offer for the publication rights to my unique ministry. My story was made into a movie, too, believe it or not. But you might not have heard of me because I wrote under a pen name. I've used the money received from the book and movie in my ministry. I have everything I want."

Walking back to the campground behind Oliver, Chad noticed that the older man's steps lagged as if reliving his unique experiences had aged him. How strange that Oliver's story resembled his own. If God wanted Oliver to travel the nation to comfort people with shattered lives, then his own situation was not as unusual as he thought.

Chad pondered several questions that were keys to his understanding of the future.

Was he feeling sorry for himself?

Was he running away from God?

If so, what did God want him to do?

When Chad and Oliver parted at the campground, Oliver put his arms around Chad and thumped him on the back.

"God bless you, Chad. God has a great future for you. Don't disappoint Him."

"You've given me a lot to think about. Have a good night's sleep."

"You, too," Oliver said as he stepped inside his camper.

Today's hike had been longer than any he had taken and Chad was overly tired, cold and hungry. He opened a can of soup and popped it into the microwave. He filled a bowl with broccoli slaw that he'd bought at the deli. He shoveled some ice cubes in a glass and filled it with cola.

It wasn't much of a meal but it satisfied Chad's hunger. He took a shower and went to bed, shivering when he heard the wind picking up and stirring the trees around his trailer. Although his mind was full of questions, he went to sleep before he could come to terms with how he could apply Oliver's story to his life. He looked forward to asking Oliver for advice on their next hike.

The sound of rain pelting the roof of the camper awakened Chad. He pulled aside the curtain above his bed and looked out on a dreary, misty morning. He slid back under the blankets, but his sleep was over.

He reached for the phone and dialed Vicky's number. When she answered, sounding sleepy, he apologized, "I'm sorry. Did I waken you?"

"No, I've been up for a half hour or so. It's raining, and I can't get enthusiastic about going out. I have volunteer work at the hospital this morning and I go to work at noon."

"It's raining here, too, and I'm wondering what I'll do. If it doesn't clear up, I may walk in the rain. Or maybe I'll just watch TV."

"There's a good football game on today."

"I don't think I'm ready for that yet." Remembering his conversation with Oliver yesterday, he questioned if he was a coward—running away from reality. Was he also running away from God, as Oliver had done?

"If the weather improves, I may take my bedroll and camp out tonight. I'll have my phone, but there are places in the forest where I can't pick up a signal. So don't be concerned if you don't hear from me."

"My prayers are with you. I have confidence that you'll soon know what you should do."

"I'm not sure about that."

He explained briefly about Oliver's ministry and how he waited on God's leading to know where to go next. "Lorene told me that God wasn't going to give me a blueprint for the rest of my life—that I'd have to learn to walk by faith rather than sight. That's what I have to accept, and it won't be easy."

"I know," Vicky agreed.

Wondering again what problems Vicky had to deal with, Chad said, "I won't keep you any longer. But we need to have a long talk soon. You still haven't leveled with me about *your* hang-ups."

"Soon, I promise. Be careful if you're hiking alone."

"I'll keep my phone with me."

Chad got up and he went through a regimen of exercises to limber the sore joints. Yesterday's steep climb had alerted him to the fact that he still wasn't in the physical condition he had been before his accident. Was the rest of his life going to be tempered by *before* the accident, *after* the accident?

Chad put a cup of water in the microwave

and moved to pull the draperies. He became instantly wide-awake, staring in astonishment at the empty lot where Oliver's camper had been. Confused thoughts and emotions rolled through Chad's mind. God had apparently told Oliver to move on. But why couldn't he at least have said goodbye? Chad had contemplated more time with this man whom he'd considered as a mentor. He was angry at Oliver and God for dangling him over a new spiritual possibility and then dropping him.

He removed the cup of water and put a tea bag in it. Seething, Chad stuck a cinnamon roll he'd bought at a deli in the microwave. He took the tea and pastry with him to the living area, elevated his feet in the lounge chair, flipped on the TV and sulked while he listened to the weather forecast that predicted an all-day rain. The pastry might have been cardboard for all the good it did him.

Vicky had put a Bible on the table beside the chair the day he'd left Columbus but Chad hadn't opened it. He picked it up, knowing that he had a problem that could only be resolved between God and himself. Vicky couldn't make the decision. Oliver couldn't have told him what to do. He had to stop depending on someone else to guide his life.

Agonized over the bitter feelings he harbored

against God, and yearning for something to remove the curtain that seemed to separate them, Chad cried out, "God, I'm miserable. What do You want me to do? Tell me. I'm ready. I've given up football. It's in the past, I accept that. Where do I go for the answers?"

The Bible fell open in his hand to the book of Jonah. How could the experiences of the Old Testament prophet shed any light on his situation? He flipped the pages to the New Testament. But he slowly returned to the book of Jonah. It had been a while since he had studied the Old Testament and he read the introduction to refresh his memory.

Jonah was a prophet whom God called to preach in the foreign city of Nineveh. Jonah was determined that he would not go as a missionary to his enemies. Deciding to flee from God's presence, he took ship in another direction. During a storm Jonah was swallowed by a big fish. Imprisoned in the fish, Jonah finally listened to God. When the fish returned him to land, Jonah went as God's spokesman to Nineveh.

For hours Chad studied the prophet's life and message, and other Scripture that dealt with humans' attempt to evade God's will for their lives. Burdened by guilt that he had been running away from God during his crisis rather than *toward* God, Chad clung to each encouraging word as a drowning man would hang on to a lifeboat. When the answer finally came, he shouted and praised God as loudly as he would have cheered in a football stadium.

We walk by faith not by sight!

Chad unfolded his long frame from the lounge chair so stiff he could hardly move. He marveled at the time that had elapsed. Suddenly he realized that he was hungry and lonely. He had to share his newfound truths with someone. Vicky was his first thought, but she was working. His parents? He thought not. Suddenly he wanted to talk to Perry, who had a doctorate in Biblical studies. Glancing at the clock on the stove, Chad saw that it would be noon in California, and he didn't want to interrupt their lunch.

He put a frozen container of lasagna in the microwave, along with two rolls for a quick lunch. He waited impatiently until he thought it was time to call Perry.

So eager was he, Chad's fingers trembled as he dialed Perry's number.

"Hi, Perry. Is this a good time to talk?"

"It couldn't be better. Lorene took Amy to

Disneyland today, along with some other mothers and toddlers from the church. I'm home alone, feeling lazy, and eager to talk to you. The sun is shining and our temperatures are in the seventies."

"Ohio is having steady rain today, and the temperatures are in the low forties. How about trading weather?"

"I wish I could share it with you. Sounds like everything is going well with you."

"I've had almost two weeks of camping and walking through the forest. It's been a great experience." He quickly filled Perry in on his improved health and his meeting with Oliver. "After all the years I've been a Christian, I feel like a dunce for needing someone to tell me what I should have known all along. I've been mad at God."

"Most of us have felt that way when we've blamed God for handing us a raw deal. More often than not it's been our own rebellion that caused the problem, although I don't consider that true in your situation."

"No, but my childish reaction to the accident was. I've spent the day looking through the Bible for an answer, focusing on the book of Jonah. I've concluded that God has something He wants me to do that no other person can do. I just don't know what it is yet."

"And you might not know for years," Perry hastened to say.

"You told me this a few weeks ago, but it really didn't sink in until today. *We walk by faith not by sight.* I'm ready to do that."

Perry chuckled and Chad knew he had pleased Perry by confiding in him. "I warn you that's a risky way to live. God might lead you places you don't want to go. I've been there, done that."

"I know I'll be frustrated because I can't see the end from the beginning, but I know that's the only direction I can go to fulfill what God wants to do in my life. I'm going back to Columbus tonight and see what happens."

"Now that you're committed to God's will in your life, you'll be surprised what He can do through you. When we offer all we have, the rest is up to God. You'll never be sorry."

"I'm looking forward to seeing you in a few weeks. We can have a longer talk then."

After he severed the connection, Chad realized that his conversation with Perry hadn't been strained at all.

Thank You, God, for restoring our friendship. Soon I'll have to deal with my lack of forgiveness over the circumstances of my birth.

Chad held the phone in his hand for several minutes wondering if he was ready to contact his friends and former teammates. With hands that trembled slightly, he dialed Tommy's number, almost hoping he would get the answering machine. But Tommy answered.

"Hi buddy. This is Chad."

A moment of silence indicated Tommy's surprise. "Man!" he finally shouted. "Am I glad to hear your voice! I pestered your father for a number where I could reach you, but he wouldn't tell me."

"I'm sorry, but I've gone through a rough time."

"I'm sure of that. Your dad said the surgery turned out good. Are you still healing?"

"Oh, I'm great physically. But I was a little slow accepting the fact that I can never play pro ball again. I didn't want to talk to anyone—especially not anyone connected with football."

A moment of silence passed before Tommy said quietly, "When I wrote you a letter and you didn't answer, I figured you blamed me for your injury."

"Not even for one minute, buddy! You know that I've never been a letter writer. I waited until I could talk to you, but that took longer than I expected. Please don't feel any guilt. I can understand how you feel because if I thought I'd caused you to be injured I'd have felt the same. The surgeon thinks that the goalpost is what caused my injury and it was the combined weight of both of us that caused it to collapse, so you aren't any more to blame than I am. Injuries are part of the risk we take when we play football—I've been hearing that ever since I started playing in Middle School."

"It just makes me feel better to talk to you and to have you sound so upbeat. What's next for you?"

"I'm not sure," Chad answered, not yet ready to talk to his friends about the renewal of his faith.

"The other guys want to hear from you."

"And I want to talk with them, but I need to get my life back on track. But tell them this— I will be at the first game of next season, so be sure you reserve the best seat in the stadium for me." He gave Tommy his phone number. "Keep in touch. Okay?"

"Of course. I feel better than I have for weeks."

After he finished speaking with Tommy, Chad hummed the tune of a gospel hymn that infiltrated his mind. Suddenly he thought of a few of the lyrics, and sang them joyfully as he made arrangements to return to Columbus and Vicky.

"One day at a time is all I'm asking from You."

* * *

Vicky was tired from her long day at the hospital and the bookstore, and her feet lagged as she walked to answer the phone that was ringing when she entered the apartment after seven o'clock.

"Hi, Vicky. It's Chad. I'm home," he said.

"Home, as at the apartment on Neil Avenue?"

"Yep. I came back today, turned in my motor home and caught a taxi to the apartment. How about going out with me for a dinner, lunch or whatever? I haven't eaten much today and I'm hungry. Maybe we could even go somewhere a little special?"

She wondered at the excitement, or was it happiness, in his voice. "Actually, I'd intended to have a boiled egg and some toast, but you've talked me into it. Give me time for a shower. You can pick me up in a half hour."

Vicky was curious about Chad's obvious change of attitude and his impulsive return to Columbus, but she didn't ask for she was convinced he would tell her tonight. She didn't think she had time to shower *and* style her hair, so she pulled on a shower cap, wondering what to wear. On her limited income, Vicky seldom bought new clothes and those were only casual garments suitable for work and church.

For once she would like for Chad to see her in something besides slacks.

She stepped out of the shower and rubbed a towel over her body while she glanced in the clothes closet. She made a face at the meager selection of clothes. There wasn't much choice—or much time! She grabbed a long black knit skirt and chose a gold crushed velour tunic to wear with it. She took a long gold chain and matching earrings from her jewelry box.

Vicky was pleased with the finished result as she surveyed her appearance in the mirror. "But what if Chad is dressed casually?" she muttered aloud. "Special" could mean anything. Had she overdressed? Over-expected?

Figuring she had made another mistake, the pleasure in her appearance dissipated arousing old fears and uncertainties. Couldn't she ever do anything right? Her misgivings increased by the minute and when Chad knocked on the door, her breath caught in her throat and her heart pounded as she opened the door.

Her fears were premature! Chad wore a dark suit, white shirt and tie.

"You look great," he said admiringly as he sauntered through the door and closed it behind him.

Laughing in relief that she had made the right choice, Vicky said, "I can return the compliment! After I put on these clothes, I decided that you might be thinking about going to a fast-food restaurant."

"Absolutely not! Only the finest tonight. We're celebrating!" Chad lifted her hand to his cheek. "A lot of things have happened to me in the past few days, but let's find a restaurant first."

He held her coat for her and followed her downstairs.

As he drove away from the apartment complex, he said, "What have you been doing?"

"Just the daily routine. This is a busy time at the bookstore. Some students are buying their books for new courses they'll be taking after Christmas. Others are shopping for gifts. And, I've had quite a few calls to sit with people at the hospital."

"I asked Grace to recommend a good restaurant, and she gave me directions to what she said was one of the best restaurants in town. We'll see."

Oh, God, don't let him take me to a restaurant I visited with Damon!

Damon's family had money, because he only took her to dinner in elegant restaurants. But he'd never taken her to the one that Chad chose. Instead of being overdressed, Vicky now wondered if her garments would be acceptable in this restaurant known as one of Columbus's most exclusive. Reservations were required but Chad had called ahead.

While the maître d' escorted them to a secluded corner of the room, Vicky concluded that it didn't matter what she was wearing because the interior was swathed in mysterious duskiness. Sconce lamps along the walls provided enough illumination to light their way but little more.

Electric candelabra on their table provided enough light for them to read the menu. They ordered lamb chops covered with citrus sauce, asparagus spears, red potatoes and Caesar salads.

Chad's eyes seemed dark and unfathomable, and it was as if a stranger shared the table with her. His black hair gleamed in the muted light. He was different tonight. His restlessness of the past few months had disappeared. She sensed a firm strength in him. For the first time Vicky felt shy in his company, questioning how much longer she would share his life.

"I've finally ended my rebellion against God," Chad said as they waited for the waiter to bring their beverages. He related the experiences with Oliver and how he had found God's will for his life as revealed in the Book of Jonah.

"I've turned the corner on my depression and doubts. I have peace in my heart that has never been there before. I'm not certain where God will take from me from this point, but I'm willing to go where He leads. I have so many decisions to make, and I don't know what to tackle first."

"Now that you're committed to let God lead the way, the next step will be easy."

"Yes, the *next* step," Chad said with a touching half smile, "but I wonder if I'll ever be sure about the ones that follow."

"Sure you will. Once you've proven that you can handle a large block of the future, God will open up His plans for you."

"It's an awesome feeling to know that God is that interested in *me*."

Their dinner was served and since both of them were hungry, they didn't talk much while they ate, though they chatted over dessert. When their dessert plates were removed, they asked for more coffee.

"That will be all for now," Chad told the waiter, for he had decided it was time for him to be the kind of friend to Vicky that she had been to him. Vicky's left arm was stretched across the table, and Chad covered her hand with his. A look of tenderness, tempered by determination, spread across his face.

"Now that I have my life turned in the right direction, isn't it time for you to tell me what happened to get you off track with God?"

Chapter Nine

Vicky stiffened at Chad's question. How could she talk to anyone about a situation she had secreted in her heart for so long? But noting the resolute determination on Chad's face, she knew he wouldn't take no for an answer.

She wanted to plead, "Not now. Don't spoil the evening."

Instead she dropped her eyes before his steady gaze and said in a voice barely above a whisper, "I guess I do owe you that."

Still she hesitated. If she told Chad the truth, he might decide he would be better off to find other companionship, and she knew that even if they were just friends it would be a blow to lose him.

But she had gnawed on her painful experience long enough, and in the few weeks she had known Chad, she had sometimes wondered if, because of her young age, she hadn't magnified the experience. Compared to what had happened to him, perhaps her mistake wasn't as bad as she remembered.

Taking a grip on her courage, she started, "For the past three years, I've been fretting over an incident that changed my outlook on the future, but it certainly doesn't compare with the trouble you've had."

"Tell me about it. Friends don't need to keep secrets from each other."

Still she hesitated to resurrect an incident she longed to forget, but was that also necessary before she renewed her vow to serve God.

"I've mentioned that I'd gone to the southern part of West Virginia as a Red Cross volunteer to clean up after a terrible flood. God had called me to be an overseas missionary, and this seemed a good opportunity to learn if I was missionary material. It was a humbling experience."

"I can understand that. My experience with the Boy Scouts in Alabama quickly changed my outlook concerning people who were having trouble."

"We worked out of a church, and even though the pastor, Allen Chambers, was several years older than I was, I fell in love with him. We were together every day. He was so kind to me I thought he shared the same feelings I did. I didn't tell him I loved him, but I'm sure I got the message across. When I learned that he was already engaged to someone else, I was shattered. It was such an embarrassing situation that I lost interest in everything, even my plans to prepare for full-time Christian service."

"Didn't you talk to anyone about this?"

"Only to my roommate, Amelia Stone. She's married now, to Chase Rause, and lives in Worthington, a few miles from here. We have lunch together occasionally, but we never discuss my crush on Allen. She knew how I felt, but perhaps she thinks I got over it." She sighed. "Maybe to some people it seems silly, but to me it was very real. The love…and the pain. After that, somehow, everything just lost meaning."

She avoided telling him of her second and worst romantic entanglement by saying, "I've been doing some soul searching, too, while you've been gone." Briefly she recounted the days she had spent driving through the country trying to make some sense of her shallow life. "I know now that God hasn't released me from the commitment I made years ago."

Chad's fingers tightened around Vicky's hand which he was still holding.

"Don't be too hard on yourself. It seems to me that every Christian is called to full-time service. Jesus didn't save us to warm a church pew on Sunday. The New Testament makes it plain that every believer has a service to perform—it might be on the mission field, in a flood-ravaged region, or in a hospital room at OSU Medical Center. I'm not sure I would have made it this far if you hadn't gone out of your way to encourage my rehabilitation. You've helped me heal in a way I wouldn't have dreamed possible when I first learned that I'd had a kidney transplant."

Vicky experienced a profound pleasure and contentment at his words. "Thank you for confirming what I felt God wanted me to do. I thought He had given me the privilege of helping you as a way to deal with my own messed-up life. When I compared my problems to yours, they didn't amount to much."

"I'm not sure about that. I've not had the experience, but I'd imagine that a shattered romance could be very demoralizing."

Chad saw the faint smile on her face fade to a brooding expression.

"To say the least," she admitted wryly, wondering if she should go ahead right now and tell him about the situation with Damon. But his face held a hint of wonder and admiration as he looked at her, and still hurting from her mother's cutting words, Vicky couldn't destroy his trust in her.

"I'm considering returning to the actual place where I dedicated myself to Christian service and take up my cross there. I also need to apologize to my Mom and Dad for disregarding their wishes and causing them so much worry the past three years. But God hasn't yet given me the grace to humble myself that much," she said with some bitterness.

"You'll have the strength to do what you know God wants you to do," he encouraged. "Now that I've surrendered my future to God, I'm not sure what my next step will be. So let's grow in faith together."

Because she thought that a good way to end an almost perfect evening, Vicky put aside the thought of telling Chad more than she had already told him. Perhaps she never would.

Chad left Vicky at her apartment, but instead of going home, he drove slowly through the quiet streets of the residential section of Columbus's Victorian Village. He was puzzled by the strange feeling that came over him when Vicky had been talking about being in love. Was he jealous of the memory she still carried of Allen Chambers? Or did he resent the man for making her unhappy? He discarded that as an unreasonable thought, when the minister probably hadn't had any idea that Vicky had a crush on him. But he didn't like to see Vicky so distressed.

And he had a strange feeling that it was up to him to protect Vicky from being hurt again. How could he best do that? As her confidant and friend? Or as her husband? He knew that marrying someone to protect them was a poor reason for matrimony. Did he love her? And did she love him? Chad was still troubled when he parked his car and climbed the steps to his apartment.

Chad relaxed in Grace's four-poster bed that was more comfortable than the one in the motor home so short he had never been able to fully stretch out his long frame. He slept later than usual, showered and dressed. He hadn't left any food in the refrigerator, and he'd forgotten to get groceries the night before. He made a cup of instant coffee, unlocked the door into the hallway and went downstairs, marveling at how much easier it was to negotiate the steps than when he had first rented the apartment.

He knocked on one of the doors. His landlady opened the door and the smell of fresh-baked bread floated into the hall. He hadn't realized how hungry he was.

"Good morning, Grace. I'm back."

She nodded. "I saw you come in yesterday afternoon. Come on in. I've got your breakfast ready. I was just going to call you."

"Maybe I've already had breakfast," he said, lifting his eyebrows inquiringly.

She answered his grin with a frown. "Humph! Have you?"

"No."

"Just as I expected," she said, smothering a smile as he followed her into the kitchen. Despite the fact that the room was large, it was one of the most cheerful places Chad had ever been.

A round table, covered with a blue-plaid tablecloth was in the center of the room. In one corner a lounge chair with a white afghan over the back faced a television. A sewing basket stood beside the chair, and a Bible was on the end table that held a reading lamp. Grace must spend most of her time in this room.

She placed a bowl of fresh fruit on the table and motioned for him to sit.

"I'll boil a couple of eggs to go with the biscuits. I take it you watch your diet."

"That's right. Biscuits are only an occasional treat. But I don't have to watch my diet this morning."

"Now that you aren't playing football, you

don't want to put on any fat. That's apt to happen," she warned.

"But I won't," he said, dipping into the fruit. "My father hasn't gained weight, but he does work out, as I intend to do regularly now that my wound has healed."

"I've had people come to the door looking for you."

"I hoped no one would know where I'm living."

"I sensed that, so I told them nothing, but I thought you should know."

"It's okay. I'm ready to come out of hiding anyway. My popularity won't last very long. Soon people will transfer their interest to athletes who are still playing ball."

Her eyes compassionate, she sat opposite him. "And you're resigned to that?"

He hesitated slightly. "Yes, I am. I never did enjoy being in the limelight. I lived to play football, but I didn't care for the notoriety. These two weeks I've been away have been good for me. I finally concluded that God has some other plan for my life rather than football. I've put my trust in the wisdom of God."

She dipped a tea bag in a cup of hot water. "That's the only way to live," she said, "but I lived a long time before I finally learned that."

"You've had your struggles, too?"

Her mouth tightened as if her memories weren't pleasant. "Losing my husband nearly killed me. Even after my husband became bedridden, I absolutely would *not* let him die. I defied the doctor's diagnosis, and knowing how I felt, my husband hung on to life long after he wanted to die. I finally realized that keeping him alive was for *me*, not for him. I was being selfish. I tried to explain that I'd released him into God's hands. He died the next day."

Grace swiped at the tears sliding down her cheeks and Chad was beside her in an instant. He knelt by her chair and put his arm around her trembling shoulders.

"And it's the same way with this house. I've lived here alone for ten years, determined to keep my memories alive. My daughter has begged me to sell the place and come live near her and the grandchildren, but I refused. I'm a stubborn old woman."

"Of course, you aren't. Maybe God had you stay on here so you could give me a home when I needed a place to live."

She patted his hand. "I wouldn't mind selling out if I knew who was buying it, but if I put the property in the hands of a Realtor, I won't have any control over what happens to it. I hate to think of the home I shared with my husband belonging to someone who didn't love and care for it as I do. I'd like to see it remain a home where people could live as a family."

"I don't know how to say this, but if you're having a financial problem now, I'd be more than happy to help you."

"You've already given me the boost I needed by leasing the apartment for six months." She retrieved a handkerchief from her apron pocket and blew her nose. "I'm all right now. Go on and finish your breakfast."

Chad stayed with Grace an hour or more, asking her questions about her husband and her family before he went to his apartment. In a further effort to deal with the present, he dialed his agent's number.

"Man! Am I glad to hear from you," Howie shouted, and Chad held the receiver away from his ear. "People have been driving me crazy— wanting to talk to you, wanting commitments from you, wanting to know where to reach you. But first, before we talk business—how are *you?*"

"Physically, I'm great. I still have a few emotional and spiritual hang-ups, but I'm mending. Thanks for being patient with me. I'm ready to talk now. I've got tons of mail that you should check through."

"Are you coming back to Pittsburgh?"

"Not now, if ever. When can you come to Columbus?"

"Tomorrow, if I can get a flight. Call you back?"

"I'll give you my new cell number. That's the only phone I have right now."

Chad met Howie at the airport the next afternoon and took him to the apartment. After the agent looked through all the mail that Chad had laid aside as important, he said, "Most of this is the same as the offers I've had. I suppose when I told them I didn't know where you were, they tried to contact you directly."

"I've already decided on things I definitely want to do, but I have questions about others. Let's hear what's number one on your list.

"You need to snap up in a hurry the offer to publish the story of your life. An athlete's public is fickle. You're still news now, but in a year you won't be. Once you're out of the limelight for a while, they'll turn to new heroes."

"I've accepted that, but I'm not sure I want a biography written."

Howie shook his head, perplexed. "I can't understand that! You have a great football record that started in high school. Why not publish a book about it? This company is also interested in movie rights on the book. They have a ghostwriter ready to hop on the project and they'll push it through to quick publication. It will make you more money than anything else offered."

"I don't care anything about the money. I'm concerned about personal issues—things I'd prefer not to have aired to the public."

"You know that unauthorized biographies can be published," Howie warned.

"That's a risk we'll have to take. I won't agree on it yet. But there are some things I want you to start working on right away, all of which will have to be approved by my accountant and lawyer. I want to establish a football scholarship at my alma mater, Wallace University, to aid underprivileged students who can't afford tuition."

He riffled through a pile of mail and pulled out an envelope. "I also want to invest a million dollars in this program designed to provide lifesaving vaccines to children in Third World countries. The information is included in this pamphlet."

He handed the pamphlet to Howie and picked up two other letters. "And I will let my name be used to promote contributions to the Red Cross and Salvation Army. I'll speak on their commercials if they want me to. You can take these letters from the two organizations to get the facts."

During their three-year association, Chad had become adept at reading Howie's reactions, and he knew his agent wasn't pleased. None of the things Chad had mentioned so far would put much money in Howie's pockets.

He fidgeted in his chair, scratched his head with his pen. "How about a half hour interview on the National Athletes network?"

"That I will do," Chad agreed readily. "I'll only be interviewed about my football career—they won't be delving into my personal life. You can arrange it when you want to."

"Will you go to the network's studio in Chicago?"

"Yes."

When Howie drew a sheaf of papers from his briefcase, Chad threw up his hands.

"Let's take a rest. I've made about all the decisions I can make at one time."

"When will you give me an answer on the book and movie?"

Chad didn't like to be pressured, but he might as well make the decision and get it out of the way. "After the Christmas holidays."

"That's not soon enough but I'll try to put the publisher off for that long. One other thing—you've been asked to endorse a new ointment designed to soothe and heal athletes' aching muscles."

"Have a sample of the ointment sent to me and to my lawyer. I'll also want to see a copy of the type of promotion they plan to release."

"Will you let me know about this endorsement before Christmas?" Howie asked hesitantly.

To see such meekness in his agent, whose nature was brusque and demanding amused Chad.

"I'll try to do that."

Chad's face spread into his normal, friendly smile. "It will all work out, Howie. Let's have dinner and then I'll take you to your hotel. We can talk again tomorrow before you leave town."

It bothered Chad that he wanted to talk to Perry and Lorene about his offers more than he did his parents. But if he allowed the story of his life to be published, he intended to tell *everything* and Lorene and Perry would be hurt more by that revelation than the Recccs. It was common knowledge that they had adopted him, but so far only a handful of people knew about his illegitimate birth.

Lorene answered his call, and he said, "Is

Perry around? I want to talk to both of you at the same time."

"Yes. He's playing horse with Amy, but I'm sure he's had enough of that. I'll get him and let Amy entertain herself for a while."

"Hi, Chad," Perry said, and he was a bit breathless. "I don't recommend waiting until you're in your fifties to become a father. Keeping up with a toddler is for a young man—not me."

"But admit you love it," Chad said, fondly thinking of his baby sister.

"I don't love crawling around on hands and knees and being kicked in the ribs by an exuberant toddler, but I love Amy and that makes it worthwhile."

"How are you?" Lorene asked.

"The doctor says I'm doing great. I spent a couple of weeks doing a lot of walking in the forest, and I feel as strong as I did before the accident. I'm ready to make some decisions now, but I need your input since it will concern your past."

"Whatever it is—we want what is good for you," Perry said. "We owe you that."

"I've been offered a deal with a major company to publish my biography, potentially with movie rights. I'm hesitant to do it because I couldn't very well suppress details about my birth. I don't want to ruin your reputations."

A silence greeted his words, and instantly he was sorry that he hadn't turned down the project.

"I won't go any further if you're opposed to it."

"I was waiting for Perry to speak," Lorene said, and there was a gentle softness in her tone. "I have no objection to having the truth come out. We made a mistake, which can't be erased. But I'd be proud for the world to know that I'm your biological mother."

"Ditto," Perry agreed. "The circumstances of your birth shouldn't be suppressed. It makes your story even more impressive because you triumphed in spite of your birth circumstances. Telling your story will encourage others who have similar problems."

"As far as we're concerned, go for it. Or are there other reasons you're hesitating?"

"It's going to put a lot more money in my pocket and I have trouble dealing with what I already have. Any advice?"

"Perry, I'll pass on that question and let you take it."

"You might put all the income from the book and movie, if it's made, into a separate account and ask God to tell you what to do with it."

"I've been thinking along that line, too." He mentioned the decisions he'd already made. "During the two weeks I was away, I put the past behind me as much as is humanly possible and promised my future to God. About the only thing He's taught me so far is that trusting Him means that I have to walk by faith."

"And no blueprint for the rest of your life?" Perry asked, and there was humor in his voice.

"Nope. Just one day at a time. I suspect that during this walk by faith, a lot of times I'll wish for the days when I went from one football season to another—knowing months in advance where I'd be."

"All of us would like that," Lorene agreed huskily. "I had no idea when I was forced to go to Woodston, to fulfill a contract to publicize their bicentennial that I'd meet Perry again, that my life would make a complete turnaround, and we would have a new life together."

"And you've never been sorry."

"Never. In a year's time, I had sold my company and became a wife and eventually a mother. That was God's plan for me all along, but I took a detour that lasted twenty years."

"If I agree to the book, when you come to Columbus in January, maybe we can agree on what we want published."

"You have the right to know everything

about your birth—and it's up to you what you want to reveal. I'm all for it."

"We're looking forward to seeing you again," Perry said.

"My landlady has a nice suite of rooms across the hall from my apartment. Her daughter's family will be staying there over the Christmas holidays, but it might be good if you could rent those instead of going to a hotel. She could use the money and we would be close together. Incidentally I have a car now, so I can meet you at the airport."

"Those arrangements would be fine. You can let us know what she says."

"Are you going to Alabama over Christmas?" Lorene asked.

"I haven't made up my mind yet, but I probably will. I'll need to discuss the biography with Mom and Dad, too, and get their opinion. I'll let you know. And hey, thanks for being so understanding."

"Thank *you* for confiding in us."

Chapter Ten

During Howie's visit Chad hadn't seen Vicky, but he called her as soon as he returned from the airport.

"Will you come over for the evening meal? I'll buy some Chinese food."

"I'd love that."

Vicky had finished work at seven and she arrived at his apartment within an hour.

"What are your plans for the holidays?" Chad asked as they ate, with the door into the hallway conveniently open for Grace's benefit.

"I'll eat Thanksgiving dinner with Mom and Dad, as usual, and by the way, Mom invited you to come, too, if you are in town."

"I'll accept. What about Christmas?"

"Mom and Dad are going to Florida to spend Christmas with her sister and attend my cousin's wedding. They're pressing me to go, too. But I'm still out of sorts with them and I suspect the trip wouldn't be very pleasant. Also, my romances have turned out to be such miserable experiences, that I wouldn't like the assembled family's comparison between me and my cousin. It would be like rubbing salt into an open wound. I'm a coward, and I'm better off staying at home. Besides, I'll be working between Christmas and New Year's getting the store inventory ready for auditing. I could work around that, but it made a convenient excuse."

Out of that long response, Chad had picked up on one word.

"Romances? Was there more than one?"

Vicky's face flushed, and she mentally kicked herself. She wasn't ready to lose Chad's good opinion by telling him about her relationship with Damon. But why put it off? She'd listened to his problems. She might as well tell him one time as another.

"There were two. Only you and Amelia Stone Rause know about the first one, but most of my friends know about the last one."

Chad's eyes were compelling Vicky to speak, but she couldn't look at him when she told him. She stood and faced the window, looking out over Neil Avenue.

Her voice was contemptuous and full of self-reproach as she told him what she had hoped he would never find out.

"Soon after I came home from the flooded area, hurting from that rejection, I fell hard for another man. That situation was what caused my mother to tell me a few weeks ago that I had no common sense where men were concerned."

Chad sensed how difficult it was for Vicky to admit this. He'd been rejected by his parents and now by the owners of his NFL team, but he had never known the rejection of someone he had loved romantically.

"So that's why you're out of sorts with your parents?"

She nodded. "It hurts even more because I know my mother was right. I don't like to admit that I acted foolishly, not once but twice within such a short time."

Chad was speechless. What was she trying to tell him? How far had this second romance gone?

"I've told you that much. I might as well finish it. Damon Steele was a graduate student at the university. We dated for over six months. He'd broken up with his girlfriend right before he came to Columbus, so both of us were on the rebound. When he returned home, he and the former girlfriend patched up their differences and got married immediately. My self-esteem hit rock bottom. I've been living in a vacuum ever since." Looking up at him, almost in defiance, she said, "It's not a pretty picture, is it?"

"But since God has asked you to take up your vow again, He isn't through with you."

"If I didn't believe that, I wouldn't have any hope. I do intend to pick up the cross again, but I'll have to forgive my parents before I can put myself in a place where God can use me."

Chad thought she also needed to forgive herself. Although he didn't see himself in the role of an advisor, he thought Vicky might listen to him.

"I don't agree with you completely. I still have to understand my parents' position in my birth and adoption, but I believe I have forgiven them. Your mother's comment was out of line, but are you sure you don't have another problem? Personally, I think your greatest obstacle is that you can't forgive *yourself*."

Vicky stared at Chad, stunned. Did he believe that her relationship with Damon had been intimate—that she had gone against her religious beliefs? Did *everyone* believe that— even her parents? If so, no wonder her mother thought she didn't use judgment in her romantic relationships! Without comment, she picked up her purse and coat. She didn't feel up to defending her virtue.

Chad followed her to the door. "Vicky, I didn't mean to make you mad. I was only trying to help."

She rushed down the stairs as if she were being chased. Chad had no idea what had caused her reaction or what he could do about it.

Vicky drove recklessly down Neil Avenue, made a rapid right and darted down the few blocks to her apartment. She slammed on the brakes and brought the car to a sudden halt. Sobbing she dropped her head on the steering wheel. What difference did it make if Chad did have questions about her purity? She didn't owe him an explanation. But why was she so angry that he doubted her? What had happened to her lofty ideals that God had called her to help effect Chad's emotional recovery? As usual, she had made a mess of her good intentions.

She cried until she was emotionally spent, got out of her car and trudged toward her apartment. Why couldn't she do anything right?

Chad didn't know how to repair the breach he'd made in his friendship with Vicky, and when he realized how empty his life would be without her, he dropped into a chair.

Exactly how did he feel about her? Were his sentiments toward her more than friendship?

With everything else that was crowding in on him now, he couldn't fall in love. And since Vicky had been involved in two disappointing relationships, he wondered if she'd risk her heart again.

But he had come to depend on Vicky. How could he make it through day after day without having her friendship? It was frightening to realize that in a matter of three months someone could have become so indispensable in his life. He would have to make it plain to Vicky that her life before they'd met was none of his business, that he liked her for who she was now.

Feeling that an apology was not the answer, he tried to think of a way to show Vicky that he approved of her without bringing up the subject directly. He had delayed calling his parents and finally thought of a way to solve his dilemma and help Vicky at the same time.

His mother answered when he called, and she asked immediately, "Are you planning to come for Christmas? You haven't been home for the holidays since you started playing for the NFL. We're looking forward to having you here. That is, if you don't intend to go to California."

"I'll be in Alabama for Christmas. And I'm wondering if you'd mind inviting Vicky Lanham to come with me. Remember, she's the one who sat with me in the hospital. Her parents will be in Florida for Christmas, and she'll be alone in Columbus. She's been so helpful to me, it would be a nice gesture to invite her to spend the holidays with us."

He sensed his mother's disappointment at not having him to herself, but he simply couldn't spend several days alone with his parents. They were bound to want answers from him about what he intended to do. Chad didn't want to be drawn into a long discussion of his blighted hopes and his uncertain future with his folks without Vicky's support. He didn't know where God was leading him yet, and he didn't want to have his parents questioning him. Vicky's presence would forestall a lot of questions.

There I go again, he thought wryly—*using Vicky for my own purposes*. Somehow he would have to get across to her that she was more than a sounding board.

"Why, of course, Chad," Mrs. Reece answered after a brief pause. "I'll be glad to call her."

Chad gave her the number. "It won't be a long visit, because Vicky won't have much time off from her job. She hasn't traveled much and I think she will enjoy some warm Alabama weather for the holidays."

"I'm sure your dad will approve, but I'll talk to him about it and call her right away."

Two days later, Vicky called Chad. "Did you ask your mother to invite me to spend Christmas with them?" She didn't sound pleased, so he supposed he'd made another mistake.

"I suggested it, yes."

"Why?"

"A selfish reason, I suppose. I figured my folks would want to talk about a lot of things I'm not ready to discuss yet, and with you there, they couldn't. But I also didn't want you to be alone in Columbus during Christmas. I hope you'll go. If you won't, then I'll stay in Columbus, too."

"But that would disappoint your parents."

"That's true, but you're at a turning point in your spiritual life now. Christmas is a down time for lots of people and even my company might be better than none. You've helped me for months and I don't want you to spend the holidays alone. Are you going?"

"I told your mother I'd have to think about it and let her know. How long will you be gone? As I mentioned, I have to work between Christmas and New Year's Day."

"We can adjust our visit to suit your work schedule. I told Mom I wouldn't be staying long. See if you can work out going on the twenty-third and coming back on the twenty-seventh?"

"Let's put my decision on hold until after Thanksgiving. You *are* going to eat with us, aren't you?"

"Yes."

With a slight laugh, she said, "Good. If you're there, *my* parents won't have an opportunity to quiz *me*."

Vicky could imagine what her mother would say about this invitation, but if she went with Chad, she wouldn't tell her parents until they got back from Florida. She would have her phone and that's the only way they could contact her anyway.

On the way home from Thanksgiving dinner with her parents, Chad asked, "Have you made a decision about going to Alabama?"

"I'll check with my boss and see if those hours will be okay. But honestly, Chad, I don't think I should go. Your mother seemed genuine in her invitation, but I know they'd rather see you by yourself."

"Maybe, maybe not. I don't know what to say to them about my injury and change of long-range plans. They might feel the same. By the way, the expenses are on me."

She laughed. "I assumed that. There's no

way I could afford a plane ticket to Alabama. If I do go, I'll try to buy a thank-you gift for your parents, but my budget will only spread so far."

In all the turmoil Chad hadn't once thought about presents. He hadn't been much of a shopper, but he decided there was no time like the present. He always gave Howie a check. He usually sent flowers to Perry and Lorene and his parents, and a toy to Amy. Since he had so much time on his hands, he might as well shop for presents this year. What could he buy Vicky? He definitely wanted to give her a gift.

He had noticed a high-end department store along High Street, south of the capitol and Grace told him the store had a wide range of items. But he waited until the Thanksgiving weekend was over to avoid the rush. Instead of driving downtown and looking for a parking place, he walked, intending to take a taxi home.

The hanging baskets along the streets were filled with greenery and artificial poinsettias. Trees on the capitol lawn were decorated with huge ornaments. Strings of lights festooned the low shrubbery and along the retaining wall bordering High Street. A huge wreath hung over the entrance to one bank, and Chad momentarily wondered how they would store such a large wreath from season to season.

The refrain of "I'll be Home for Christmas" greeted Chad's ears as he walked through the heavy glass doors of the store. He went to the toy department first and, on the advice of one of the clerks, bought some picture books, a Cinderella doll and a set of educational videos for Amy. He carried the items to the customers' center to be wrapped while he continued shopping.

He wandered through the jewelry and cosmetic department of the store, and then to the ladies clothing section. He wished he'd brought Grace along to help him choose something for Vicky. He was about to leave the store and come back another day when a matronly looking clerk approached him. She had an amused gleam in her eye and Chad wondered if she'd been watching him.

"Can I be of any help?" she asked kindly.

He laughed. "It must be obvious that I need help. I want to buy a gift for my parents and for a good friend."

"Is this a 'special' friend or just a friend?"

He colored a little. "She is special, but not in the way you're suggesting. She's helped me out of some very rough situations in the past three months, and I want to get her a nice gift. Kind of a thank-you gift. But I don't know what's appropriate for me to buy her. Cosmetics, jewelry, clothes?"

"Do you know what size clothes she wears?"

He shook his head.

"Gloves, scarves and accessories are always nice choices. Could you describe her to me? Let's start with her eyes."

"They're blue, sort of like the sky at sunrise. And she's got long lashes a little darker than her hair."

The clerk took a notepad from her pocket and made notes. "And what color is her hair?"

"Brown. About like yours. It's long, down to her shoulders. A little curl in it, too. Her skin looks like pearls."

The clerk's lips trembled with the need to smile.

"Are you laughing at me, ma'am?"

Her smile deepened. "A little. But you've given me a good description."

"She's taller than average," he said as she motioned for him to follow her. He measured a place an inch or two below his shoulder. "She comes up to about here on me."

This time the clerk exploded into laughter and Chad decided it was time to stop his descriptions.

"Let's find something for your friend first, then we'll buy for your mother. Let's rule out cosmetics since you don't know what she likes. You could buy perfume for her but that, too, can be risky. Some people are allergic to certain scents. I'd suggest gloves and scarves or jewelry for both your friend and your mother. What price range are you interested in?"

He shrugged his shoulders. "The price doesn't matter—if it's something I think they want. But I don't think gloves and scarves sound very exciting. I never did like to get clothes as presents."

"Does your friend wear jewelry?" He nodded.

"Earrings?"

"Yes—her ears are pierced."

"Aha! Now we're getting somewhere. Let's go to the jewelry department."

"Since we're in the clothing department, I'll buy a scarf and gloves for Vicky, then we'll get some jewelry. And while I'm at it, I'll buy a gift for my mother, too. Am I taking up too much of your time?"

"Of course not."

Since the woman was much the size and age of his mother, she suggested a suitable sweater for her, as well as gloves and a scarf. After fidgeting around he bought a matching set of white gloves, a scarf and a hat for Vicky.

As they approached the jewelry department,

he said, "I don't know any more about jewelry than I do about women, but I think her earrings are inexpensive. I'd like to buy something *really* nice. Show me some diamond earrings."

He noticed that the clerk showed some surprise when he chose a pair of one carat diamond earrings without even asking the price, but she said nothing. After he bought several books and a nice sweater for his father, he gave his helper a twenty dollar bill for being so nice and took his purchases to be gift wrapped.

Next Chad went to the electronics department to buy a television for Grace. He had noticed that her television set was old and that the screen was small. The clerk assured him that it would be delivered a few days before Christmas.

Vicky arranged for a poinsettia to be sent to Chad's parents. And wondering what a pauper like her could buy for a multimillionaire, she pondered long over a gift for him. If she bought something at the bookstore, with her employee's discount, she could buy a better gift than she could afford in another store. She settled on a devotional desk calendar with a special message for each day of the year. That would be easy for him to take with him no matter where he lived, and she could easily tuck it into her luggage.

On the day before they left for Alabama, Vicky had second thoughts about telling her parents that she was going with Chad. To repair the damaged relations with her parents, she had to start now.

Fortunately for her, her father answered the phone.

"Merry Christmas, Dad."

"Merry Christmas yourself. We just came from a long walk along the beach. The weather is wonderful. What's it like in Columbus?"

"Temperature in the teens, about an inch of snow on the ground and a strong north wind," she said, laughing.

"We miss you. I wish you were here with us."

It was easier to talk to her father than her mother, and she said, "Just between us, I couldn't face the combined family right now. I wouldn't have enjoyed the wedding, thinking that everyone would be feeling sorry for me."

"I understand, and that's the reason I didn't insist on you coming. But we've never been separated before on Christmas. I don't like for you to be alone."

"That's one reason I called, Dad. I won't be alone. I'm going with Chad to his parents' home in Alabama. His mother called to invite me—remember, I met his parents when he was in the OSU Medical Center? We're leaving tomorrow morning and will be back the day after Christmas. If necessary you can contact me on my cell phone."

"Do you want me to tell your mother where you are?"

"Use your own judgment. If it will spoil the holidays for her, don't say anything. But I thought you should know where I am."

"Thanks for letting me know. I may not tell her until we start back home."

"I love you."

"And we love you, too. And in spite of what you might think, we do have faith in you. Your mother gets worried now and then, but we'll always support any decision you make."

"Thanks, Dad. That's the best Christmas gift you could have given me."

Chapter Eleven

Now that Vicky had agreed to go with him to Alabama, Chad was looking forward to going home for Christmas. Freed from much of the pressure that had been his constant companion for weeks, he anticipated a good visit.

The day before their departure, Howie called and reported that plans were going forward with the football scholarship in Alabama, as well as the endorsements Chad had approved. The accountants and his lawyer, however, were encountering a lot of red tape that had to be resolved before his gift to the children of Third World countries would be finalized.

"Let me know your answer about the book when you get back in Columbus," the agent said, "because the publisher is eager to contact you."

"I'll do that. While I'm at home I'll gather

scrapbooks and other items Mom has kept through the years."

"I'm sure the publisher will send a ghost-writer and photographer to your hometown, too, so clear that with your folks."

Vicky had finally put aside her misgivings about the propriety of going to Alabama with Chad, and she eagerly anticipated the opportunity to see more of the country than Ohio and its neighboring states. Her flying experience was relatively limited, and the night before they were to leave, excitement and anxiety kept her awake for hours. The crash of a plane in California the week before had reminded her of the dangers of flying.

Chad decided to leave his car at the apartment building, and he called for her in a cab at five o'clock. They had an eight o'clock flight, but the taxi delivered them to the Delta loading gate in a half hour. Chad, an experienced traveler, directed Vicky how to use the automatic check-in. He had cautioned her in advance to be sure that she had her drivers' license for identification and had mentioned items that shouldn't be placed in her carry-on bag.

The check-in went off without a hitch, but Vicky fidgeted as they waited in line to go through security.

Noting Vicky's serious expression and tense fingers clutching her purse strap, Chad put his arm around her shoulders and pulled her close in a brief hug.

"This is all routine searching. Don't be upset."

"I know it's to our advantage that they *are* so particular, but I'm a little nervous about flying. This doesn't help."

"I'll take care of you and you'll have a good time. I promise you."

Vicky held her breath and walked carefully as she approached the arched security gate. She passed through without incident and flashed Chad a smile over her shoulder. She gathered her coat, purse and carry-on bag after they cleared the security camera and waited for Chad, who wasn't detained, either.

They stopped for a breakfast of rolls and juice in a small café before they went on to their departure gate.

"Thanks for asking me to go with you," Vicky said. "I shouldn't have barged in on a family Christmas observance, but I think it will be fun."

"You didn't barge in—we invited you, remember? We'll adopt you for the next few days, so just pretend you're a Reece."

Wide-eyed, Vicky stared at him a moment

before she cast her eyes downward. She had no idea what to make of the speculative gleam in the smoldering depths of his eyes.

"And stop worrying that you aren't welcome. Mom will be tickled to have another woman around the house so she won't be outnumbered."

And Vicky did feel better when both Mr. and Mrs. Reece met them at the Birmingham airport. If they were displeased that she had come, Vicky couldn't tell by their warm greeting. After they retrieved their luggage from the carousel and walked to the parking garage, Mr. Reece inserted a key into a new SUV.

Chad shouted with laughter when he saw it and circled the shiny maroon vehicle with interested eyes and gestures.

"Dad! You finally gave up that old truck you've been driving for years."

Mr. Reece grinned sheepishly. "Not really. I kept it to drive around town. I bought this for Betty's Christmas gift."

"Way to go!" Chad said, obviously pleased.

Vicky remembered that he had put a large portion of his NFL signing bonus in trust for his parents' use, which must have encouraged them to buy a new vehicle. Vicky looked at Chad with new admiration. He was always talking about how fortunate he was that the

Reeces had adopted him. Vicky thought the shoe might be on the other foot. In her opinion, the Reeces had struck gold when they adopted Chad.

The Reeces' home was located in a town of five thousand people, a two-hour drive from Birmingham. Since they'd stopped en route for lunch, when they reached the town, Mr. Reece drove up and down several streets with Chad pointing out to Vicky the places that had molded his childhood. The elementary school. The football field where he'd played in his first game. The grocery store, where Mr. Reece had worked for years, and where Chad had earned his first money.

"There's where I bought a bicycle with the money I'd worked all summer to save," he said as they passed a hardware store.

"Drive past the church, too, Stewart," Mrs. Reece said. "We'll go there for a midnight service on Christmas Eve." The church was a white frame building and the sign over the door gave the construction date at 1945. "It was built soon after World War II ended. That's where Stewart and I were married."

The Reeces lived in a bungalow-style home with dark green siding and white trim. Window boxes with blooming pansies were on the windows on either side of the front porch. Mr.

Reece drove behind the house and parked beside a faded blue pickup. A white gazebo stood in the center of a well-kept lawn.

"Excuse us for taking you in the back door," he said, "but that's the way we always go in. We want you to feel at home."

"My parents go in their back door most of the time, too."

"Show her around, Mom," Chad said, "while I bring in our luggage. Our home is almost as unique as the Victorian homes along Neil Avenue—on a more modest scale, of course."

"This is a Sears 'house-in-a-box,'" Mrs. Reece explained. "Do you know why they are unique?"

Vicky shook her head. "No, but I'm sure I've heard of them."

"They were house kits sold by Richard Sears, the man who founded the Sears Roebuck mail-order company. Starting in 1895, for a period of forty or fifty years he sold precut house kits. Every item the home builder would need came in the kits. This house was built in the mid-twenties."

Chad came in with the luggage and put his in a downstairs room. He set Vicky's two bags near the stairway.

"These houses were available in all sizes," he said. "A house like ours could be bought for less than a thousand dollars. But large Georgian Colonials and Victorian models as big as Mrs. Lashley's home were available too."

"There were six rooms on the first floor in the original plan, which included three bedrooms," Mrs. Reece continued, "but we renovated the house twelve years ago, took out some partitions and made a large bedroom for us. We raised the roof and added a bathroom and another bedroom upstairs for Chad."

"That's where you're going to sleep," Chad said. "I asked Mom to put you in my room so you can have your own bathroom. I'll take your luggage up now, and you can go along if you want to see where you'll be sleeping. I've got the guest room."

"I'm going to start dinner," Mrs. Reece said. "Please let me know if there's anything you need."

At the top of the stairs, they entered a large room with a slanted ceiling dominated by a football theme. The bedspread was covered with football scenes and a wide border along the ceiling matched it. The curtains were made of similar fabric.

"Mom hasn't changed this since I left home," Chad said apologetically. "I've tried to tell her that I won't be living here again and that she should change the decor but she hasn't."

"Mothers are like that. My bedroom at home is the same as it was three years ago when I left."

A glass-enclosed cabinet along one wall held numerous football trophies, and as Vicky's gaze roved over them, once again she was struck with the tragedy of Chad's injury. Would coming into the room remind him again of the change in his life?

He placed her bags on a padded bench at the foot of the bed. Shoulders rigid he stood like a statue in the middle of the room. His expression was tight with pain and his eyes clouded with visions of the past.

Should she ignore his trauma?

Chad sat on the foot of the bed, took a deep breath and closed his eyes. Timidly, Vicky put her arms around his shoulders and nestled her head against his. Her throat was tight and she couldn't say anything. After a heart-wrenching moment, Chad pulled her around to sit beside him and kept his arm around her waist.

His brows drew together in an agonized expression, his mouth was tight and grim, and a few tears trickled down his face. With the tips of her fingers, Vicky wiped them away.

"I'm so sorry," she whispered.

Taking a deep breath, he said, "I know you

are. I thought I was over it—thought I'd accepted what had happened to me. But walking into this room emphasized my shattered hopes and dreams. I couldn't handle it."

"It's only natural that you'd feel that way. The first time home after your injury was bound to be difficult."

"I expected it to be difficult, but I wasn't prepared for the stab of pain that seared my heart." He shook his head as if he needed to clear his thoughts. "I have to get over this in a hurry. I can't have Mom and Dad see the way I am now."

"They'll understand."

"Yes, they will, but it will worry them, and I've caused them enough pain already."

Chad put both arms around her, and she felt his uneven breathing on her forehead as he held her close.

"And here you are again when I need you so much. Will I ever get over my dependence on you? Someday maybe I can find the words to tell you how much I appreciate you."

A knot rose in her throat and she made no attempt to answer him. She hoped he couldn't feel the hammering of her heart against her ribs. Vicky stored up this sensation of being in his arms for the day that was bound to come when Chad would no longer need her.

He held Vicky away from him, searching her face, trying to read her thoughts. Her earnest blue eyes studied him for a moment before she lowered her lashes. Sighing, he leaned forward and kissed her closed eyes then put her gently away.

"You may want to hang up your clothes and settle in. The bathroom is to the left of the stairway. Come back downstairs when you're ready."

Although the Reeces didn't seem to be putting forth any big effort to entertain her, it wasn't long before Vicky felt completely at ease with both of them. If they hadn't wanted her to make this visit, they certainly hid it well. Vicky helped Mrs. Reece clear away the dinner dishes and fill the dishwasher before they went into the family room to watch some clips of Chad's early days playing football. Apparently he had gotten over the earlier discomfort for he discussed the games freely with his father.

After an hour, Vicky pushed forward to the edge of her chair. "If you'll excuse me," she said, "I'll go to my room. I've worked long hours the past two days to catch up on my duties so I could make this visit, and I'm tired."

"Why, of course," Mrs. Reece said. "I'll

come with you to be sure that you have everything you need. I want to show you where extra towels are."

As he knew she would do, as soon as his mother returned to the living room, she sat beside Chad on the couch and took his hand.

"Now tell us. How are you? We don't want you to talk about anything that upsets you, but we need to know for our own peace of mind."

"Betty, give the boy time," his father said. And he added, "Don't let her rush you, son."

Chad attempted to conceal the slight annoyance he felt at her probing. He did owe them an explanation.

"I haven't intentionally kept you in the dark, but it isn't easy to discuss the experiences of the past several weeks over the phone."

Chad stood and wandered around the room, much as he had done when he was in high school, especially after his team had lost. He told them of his disillusionment, his two weeks of wandering in the state park trying to find his way.

"I started to heal when I finally accepted my changed status and stopped blaming God for what had happened. My trouble was that I couldn't think of the blessings I had because I was too set on feeling sorry for myself. Perhaps I shouldn't have brought Vicky with me, but we owe a lot to her. I could talk to her about my feelings when I couldn't talk to anyone else. She could understand because she's had a lot of disappointments, too."

"Your friends have always been welcome here, as you know," Mrs. Reece said. "And although Vicky is the first *girl*friend you've brought home, we're glad she came. It made it much easier for us to leave you in Columbus because you were acquainted with her."

Chad couldn't decide how much emphasis his mother had given *girl*friend so he let the comment pass.

Because his parents were involved in his will, he tried to keep them abreast of his investments. He told them of his meeting with Howie and the endorsements he had made, and about the book and movie offer.

"This is one decision I won't make without input from you and Perry and Lorene. They're coming to Columbus in January so Perry can be checked by the surgeon, and I'll have this same discussion with them. If I approve having my life's story written, it's going to start with my birth. How much are you willing to have revealed?"

"It's no secret that you were adopted," his father said. "And there certainly isn't anything about your childhood to be ashamed of. They can publish anything."

"You took me when I was a week old, so as far as I was concerned, I didn't have any life before that. I didn't want to talk about my adoption. I wasn't even curious. But tell me a little about that now. Why did you choose to adopt?"

"Because it seemed that was the only way we could ever have a child," his mother said. "We didn't marry until we were in our midthirties, and after two miscarriages, we approached adoption agencies. That wasn't as easy as we'd hoped because we were in our forties by then, and most agencies prefer to find a home for babies with young couples. We could have had any number of older children, but we were set on having an infant."

"Then we had the opportunity to adopt you," Mr. Reece said. "Lorene's father was the one pushing the adoption and he wanted it done as quickly as possible, fearing Lorene would change her mind. We were the only parents our agency had who met the requirements for immediate adoption. It happened so fast, it was like a dream come true."

"It was the proudest moment in our lives when we brought you home, and you've never given us cause to regret it. You came from good stock from your parents and heredity does have an impact on the outcome of a child."

"Yes, but thanks to you, I had a good home environment, too. I've never regretted having you for my parents, either."

"We didn't meet Lorene during the adoption, and I think you should know that she held out for several days. But her father was too strong-willed for her. We were watching through a window when her father took you from her arms. I've never forgotten how she cried! That haunted me for months. I felt so mean taking her baby, for I believe, if given the opportunity she would have been a wonderful, caring mother."

Chad's gaze suddenly clouded with tears, and he cried as he had never done in his life. If any resentment still remained in his heart against his biological parents, his tears washed the slate clean.

For the remainder of their visit, Vicky saw to it that Chad had a few hours alone with his parents each day. Part of that time she walked around the small town enjoying the warm climate, the blooming flowers, green grass and birdsong that weren't a part of Columbus's winter landscape.

Other times, she stayed in her room reading, but more often she found herself looking at the mementos of Chad's life before she knew him. She returned again and again to stand before the small oval school pictures of Chad—from the time he entered kindergarten until he graduated from high school. Mrs. Reece had grouped them together in a large frame.

Now that Chad had come to terms with the changes in his life and his physical, emotional and spiritual healing was almost completed, Vicky was convinced that he would soon go out of her life. That was one reason she had agreed to make this trip to Alabama with him. God obviously had great things in mind for Chad that would take him far from Columbus. Vicky must realize that the time loomed closer and closer when Chad and she would take different paths. In her heart she was storing up memories to last a lifetime.

After a light supper of soup and sandwiches on Christmas Eve, the Reeces gathered in the family room to open gifts in their customary manner. The poinsettia Vicky had ordered was delivered on December twenty-fourth, and Mrs. Reece was obviously pleased with it. Their gift to Vicky was a set of bath and body lotions, which she considered a luxury for she couldn't afford that quality on her budget. Vicky was also pleased with the scarf, hat and gloves Chad bought for her. He really liked the gift she'd given him.

At eleven o'clock they walked three blocks to the Reeces' church. The small candlelit building was filled to capacity by the time the informal service started. The congregation sang favorite carols upon request. A trio of young women sang, "O Holy Night," prior to the pastor's message. He focused on Mary's willing response to the Angel's message that she would become the mother of the Messiah.

The minister closed with the words, "And the call goes out to all of us tonight. When God calls us to a particular task, will we, like Mary, be able to say, 'I am the Lord's servant. May it be to me as you have said'?"

Chad reached for Vicky's hand and squeezed it, and she sensed that, as she had, he had accepted the words as a personal commitment. He continued to hold her hand throughout the closing hymn and the benediction.

During the time Chad was alone with his parents they talked over the intimate details of his childhood years. These hours with his parents convinced Chad that they had set him free to do what he wanted to do.

He had delayed telling them about his spiritual experiences with Oliver and how God had dealt with him until they were at the airport ready to go back to Columbus.

"I've put myself at God's disposal," he said. "I'm His ambassador—willing to do what He wants me to do and go where He wants me to go, no matter what it costs me in money, or even if it takes my life."

"We're behind you in whatever decisions you make," his father assured him. "You've never done anything yet that hasn't made us proud of you, and you won't in the future."

"Please forgive my attitude of the past two months and my rejection of you right after the accident. I shouldn't have done that, and I'm sorry."

"You were hurting so much—it was a normal reaction," Mrs. Reece said.

When they said goodbye before Chad and Vicky went through security, Mr. and Mrs. Reece hugged Vicky and insisted that she was welcome to return at any time. Chad held both his father and mother in a strong embrace to say goodbye. He wondered if they sensed, as he did, that this parting was different from all others. Whatever God had in mind for his future would supersede the loyalty he had to them. Tears blinded his eyes as he followed Vicky down the skyway.

* * *

After they'd arrived in Alabama, Chad had decided to let the hat, scarf and gloves pass as his only gift for Vicky. He believed he had convinced his parents that he and Vicky were platonic friends, which they might have questioned if they saw the expensive earrings he'd bought for her. He put the small box in his carry-on luggage when he packed to leave, but after they went through security, he put the box in his coat pocket.

They had a long walk to reach their departure gate, and when they passed a waiting area that was empty, Chad said, "We have plenty of time to reach the gate before the plane takes off. Let's sit here for a few minutes." They found seats that looked out over the busy runways. He took the box from his pocket.

"I still have one gift to give you," he said. He didn't make any explanation as to why he hadn't put it under the tree in his parents' home. How could he when he wasn't even sure himself?

"I hope you like it," he said, handing the box to her.

For one poignant moment she wondered if he was giving her a ring and what her reaction would be if it was. She was so relieved when she saw the earrings instead of a ring that she didn't protest the expensive gift.

"They're beautiful. Thank you."

"I don't know anything about jewelry," he said nervously. "Are they the kind you can use?"

"Yes, of course."

She immediately removed the large gold hoops she wore and replaced them with his stunning gift. She inspected the gift by looking in a small compact mirror she carried in her purse. The earrings were quite a step up from her usual jewelry, but her parents had taught her as a child to be gracious when people gave her something and not to depreciate their kindness with a negative response. In this instance, it wasn't a comfortable policy to follow.

"They're beautiful. Thank you. And thanks for inviting me to come home with you. I feel as if I know you a lot better now than I did before. Your parents were lovely to me. I don't know about you, but I rather dread going back home—not knowing what's waiting for us in the future."

"This is the saddest I've ever been to leave home. Always before home was an anchor for me, but this trip cut the apron strings. I'll go back, of course, but only for visits. It's time

I put my personal roots down, established a home of my own."

"And you don't want to do that in Alabama?"

He shook his head, and he was silent most of the way to Memphis. Realizing that Chad was contemplating his future, Vicky looked out the window, enjoying the changing landscape below, yet wondering how his decision would affect her.

Chapter Twelve

Chad left his apartment and ran down the steps to knock on Grace's door. He heard her call from the laundry room at the end of the hallway and he headed in that direction. His landlady was removing clothes from a dryer.

"Hi," he said, and he leaned over and picked up a towel to fold. "I got home last night."

"I thought I heard water running up there about midnight. Did you have a good visit with your parents?"

"Yes. How about your Christmas?"

"Good. My family left yesterday and I feel awful lonesome today."

"How would you like to have some more company then?"

She slanted a suspicious glance toward him. "How's that?"

"My friends from California are coming to

Columbus next week. Perry is the one who donated the kidney that saved my life, and the surgeon wanted him to come back for a checkup. They have a daughter who's almost three now. If your rooms across the hall from mine are going to be vacant, I thought you might want to rent them for a week to Perry and Lorene. I could see them more often that way, and you could take in some extra money."

"Sounds all right to me," she said. "When will they be here?"

"Five days from now. I'm sorry I didn't let you know sooner, but I wasn't sure when they would be here."

She shrugged off this apology. "No problem. That will give me plenty of time to get the rooms ready. I've even got a child's bed that my granddaughter uses. Will they use the bathroom in your apartment?"

"Yes, no problem there."

"They can also have access to the powder room on this floor, too," she said, taking a towel from his hands and refolding it.

"They'll agree to whatever is convenient for you." Favoring her with a pert look, he picked up another towel to fold.

"Had your breakfast?"

"Such as it was."

"Which means you didn't have anything fit to eat! Do you want me to fix your breakfast?"

"Yes. I'm afraid that two-week-old bagel and a cup of coffee won't last me long." He laughed.

"Come in. I've already eaten, but I had French toast and there's still some batter left."

He followed her into the kitchen that was cozy and cheerful in spite of an overcast sky that kept the sun from shining in the windows over the sink.

"My daughter and I had words before she left," she said as she turned on the heat under the skillet.

"You mean you quarreled?"

"Not exactly, but she's annoyed with me because I won't move closer to her. The older kids want to stay home for Christmas, but she thinks she should come to see me. Her husband had to work and he didn't even come, so their family was separated."

"And that made you feel guilty? Have you ever considered going to visit them on Christmas?"

"I'm afraid to fly."

"So you're at an impasse with your daughter."

"Yes. I've insisted that she just stay home for Christmas and forget about me, but she won't do it."

"Is it Columbus you don't want to leave? Or this house?"

"The house. I've always lived in this city and I would hate to move. But the house has been in our family for years. All my memories are wrapped up in these walls."

"You could make new memories."

"Maybe. I did tell her I'd think about it. I wouldn't mind so much if I could be sure that the people who bought my home would take good care of it."

While he ate his breakfast, Grace quizzed him about his visit. She reported that they had snow on Christmas Day, which was a far cry from the seventy-degree temperatures they'd enjoyed in Alabama.

After he went back to his apartment, Chad started thinking about Grace's problem and his need to establish a permanent place of residence. Was it logical for him to live in Ohio when his parents were in Alabama? A few years from now, he might have to provide a home for them. And was this huge house a good choice for a bachelor? But he was almost sure that he didn't want to remain a bachelor— that would depend on Vicky.

Chad parked his car in the garage adjacent to Columbus International Airport, and with springing steps, walked across the main terminal. He had an hour to wait before the plane arrived from California. He was looking forward to seeing Perry and Lorene. When he'd told them goodbye in the OSU Medical Center, his spirits were so low he wasn't sure he would ever want to see them again. Time had changed many things, including his attitude toward his biological parents.

He took the escalator to the second floor and stopped for lunch in the restaurant near the entrance to the gates. He finished his lunch and had a forty-five-minute wait before their plane's arrival was announced.

Lorene exited security first, carrying Amy, and he called to them. Perry followed, his hands full of their luggage.

"It's sure great to see you," Chad said, hugging Lorene around the shoulders.

Amy held out her arms. "Chaddie! Chaddie!" she cried, and he took her from Lorene.

"Hello, sweetie," he said, smiling warmly at his baby sister.

"Yes, and she's nearly driven us out of our minds all the way across the continent by saying it every five minutes or so," Perry said, putting the luggage on the floor.

Chad kissed Amy on both cheeks and handed her back to Lorene and shook hands with Perry.

"I'll help Perry with the bags," he said. "We'll take the escalator to the first floor where we can pick up the rest of your things. Did you have a good flight?"

"It was smooth flying," Perry said.

"We saw lots of snow as we crossed the Southern Rockies and the plains."

"We have a little snow on the ground," Chad said, "and more is predicted, so you may see some here, depending on how long you can stay."

"Having lived in the Northeast for most of my first forty years, I've seen all of the snow I want to," Lorene said. "But it would be fun for Amy to be able to play in it."

"I've made arrangements for your housing with my landlady as I mentioned," Chad explained as they waited for the luggage to be unloaded. "I thought it would be more fun for you to be right across the hall, rather than going back and forth to a hotel. You can use my car, Perry, when you go to the surgeon."

"I can rent a car," Perry said, "if you need yours."

"I don't use a car often. I still go to the well-ness center at OSU, but I've been walking or running up there. It's several blocks away, but I want to keep in shape."

"You're looking so good," Lorene said, with

admiring eyes, "it's hard to imagine what has happened to you."

"God has been good. He's not only given back my health but I'm healing otherwise, too. I'm scheduled to have my first television interview in Chicago the middle of January. If that turns out all right, I think I'll be able to put the past behind me and focus on the future."

Lorene and Perry had seen very little of Columbus during their traumatic trip when Chad had been injured, and Lorene, in particular, was delighted with the Victorian homes on Neil Avenue.

"What a lovely street! It's almost like we've gone back a century."

"I feel like that late at night when the traffic is almost at a standstill and a fog settles in and dims the electric lights. Quite a few of the residents walk then, and I have occasionally."

Instead of going around the house to park, Chad stopped along the street. "It'll be easier to take in the luggage through the front door. I'll introduce you to Grace first and let you see your rooms."

Perry had been sitting in the rear with Amy strapped in the car seat Chad had rented so they wouldn't have to bring one with them. He stepped out, opened the door for Lorene and unbuckled Amy. By that time Grace was standing on the front porch, and Chad was reminded of the time he'd come looking for an apartment. Grace had seemed formidable, intimidating then—not the friend she was today.

After the introductions, Grace said, "Chad, you can show your friends upstairs. I've taken the liberty to provide a meal for you. After a long flight, I didn't think you'd want to be going out for dinner."

Chad hugged her. "That's nice of you. But I know your real reason—you were afraid I'd try to cook for them. Now admit it!"

She shook off his embrace. "Humph! I'll have the food ready in an hour if that suits you."

"We appreciate that, Mrs. Lashley," Perry said. "I believe Chad found a good place to live."

"But you won't believe how she bullies me," he protested.

Turning on her heel and heading toward the kitchen, Grace threw a glance over her shoulder and had the last word. "You've been such a challenge to me."

After dinner, Lorene put Amy in the bed that Grace had provided. She left the doors open between their quarters so she could hear if Amy wakened and then joined Chad and Perry in his living room.

"We need to pay Grace for that meal, Perry," she said. "It was delicious."

"I think you'd insult her if you even offered," Chad answered. "I'll think of some way to help her—maybe invite her to go out for dinner with us some evening. She might like that. Sometimes when Vicky is here she comes upstairs and eats with us."

"Vicky?" Lorene said.

"Oh, I'd forgotten that Mom and Dad know Vicky, but you don't. Vicky Lanham does volunteer work at the hospital and she sat with me several nights after my surgery. After all of you left, she was the only one I knew here, and she's been wonderful. She found this apartment for me and she drove me around Columbus until I rented a car. Mom invited her to spend Christmas with us in Alabama and she did. If she isn't working, we'll have lunch together tomorrow.

"And since you won't ask, I'll add that you shouldn't place any significance on our association. At this point, we are friends and nothing more. I don't know what the future holds."

"It's so hard not to give you advice unless you ask for it," Perry said plaintively.

"Oh, jump right in," Chad said with a laugh. "I'm so used to it from Grace that I take all advice and criticism in my stride."

"If you do fall in love with Vicky, or someone else, don't wait for twenty years like Lorene and I did to get married. The past three years have been the happiest of our lives."

"Strange as it might seem, I'm happy, too. I can watch a football game and sports network now without any hint of remorse. I'm actually looking forward to the interview in Chicago."

Lorene walked across the hall to check on Amy, and when she returned, Chad told them about the interviews he'd agreed to and the contributions he'd made to various charitable organizations.

"When I went home for Christmas, Mom and Dad gave their go-ahead for the publication of my biography. And to use my discretion on what I wanted to tell. Now we must discuss how this book would affect you. Or would you rather wait until tomorrow when you aren't so tired?"

"We have had a long day," Perry said, "but our bodies are still on Pacific time, so we won't go to sleep for a while yet."

"We don't expect you to suppress our youthful love for each other, or even the fact that I put you up for adoption. That's part of your life, which might have turned out much worse if I'd kept you and tried to raise you as a single parent. The Reeces gave you what I couldn't at that time—security."

"As I mentioned to you on the phone, I can't decide what to do with the money I'll receive on the book. I have more now than I need. Whenever I give away a large sum, what I have left seems to multiply. I'm praying for God to reveal a project to spend that money on."

"He will."

"In the meantime, I feel like I need to put down some roots. I lived in Alabama when I went into college, then in Pittsburgh during my NFL career, but I don't want to make my permanent home in either of those places. When the lease runs out on the apartment in Pittsburgh next month, I won't renew it. But I feel like I'm drifting around somehow."

"Are you asking for advice?" Perry said grinning.

"Not really—I'm just thinking out loud." His brows shot up in amusement. "Were you going to suggest California?"

"No." Perry sighed. "Now that I've retired from my university post, we don't have any reason to stay in California. If we move, it will be somewhere east of the Mississippi. My parents live in Illinois and Lorene's live in New Jersey now. We want to be somewhere so Amy won't have to go clear across the continent to visit any of her grandparents."

"Why don't you come to Columbus? That would be about halfway between your parents."

Lorene lifted her eyebrows. "Are you serious?"

"Yes. I've sort of fallen in love with Columbus, and this house in particular. I might buy it."

"What does Mrs. Lashley think about that?"

"I haven't asked her," Chad said, a mischievous gleam in his eyes. He explained about his landlady's financial status and her daughter's desire to have her mother closer.

"Her grandparents built this house, and it's always been in the family. She won't sell, fearful it won't be taken care of or that the wrong people might buy it. She likes me—I think she will sell to me."

"It's such a large house for one person."

"I doubt that Grace will sell it to me unless I promise to get married and raise a family," he joked, but he could tell the way Lorene looked at him that she thought he was being serious. "If I did that, you'd want to be close to your grandchildren, wouldn't you? And I'd like to see my sister grow up."

Perry and Lorene exchanged hopeful glances. Perhaps they were wondering if this was his way of telling them that he'd forgiven them for the unsavory circumstances of his birth. But Chad wouldn't leave them to wonder.

"I suppose this is a good time to apologize for my childish behavior in the hospital when you saved my life. While I was home over Christmas I apologized to Mom and Dad and tried to make them understand how much I appreciate what they did for me. So I'm telling you now—I love both of you. I'm fortunate to have two sets of parents I can be proud of."

Lorene started crying and Chad leaped out of his chair to kneel beside her. "I didn't mean to make you cry."

"I often cry when I'm happy, and you've made me happier than any other time in my life except the day Perry and I were married. We sort of lost our way, but God, in His goodness, brought us together and has reunited us with you."

Perry cuddled Lorene into his arms. "More than anything else, I'm thankful that you actually want us to live close to you. We don't deserve that, but since we missed the first quarter of your life, we would like to be close enough to share the rest of it."

"I don't expect you to make a decision right now, because I don't know for sure that living in Columbus is God's plan for me. And

Grace might surprise me and not let me have her home. But even if I can't buy this house, there are other places that I like."

Grace declined to go out for dinner with them, but he called and asked Vicky to go with them the next night. Over the phone Chad filled Vicky in on his reconciliation with Perry and Lorene and even mentioned that all of them might settle in Columbus. He couldn't tell if Vicky was pleased or not. Before they went to Alabama, her opinion about his settling in Columbus wouldn't have made that much difference to him, but their relationship had changed during those five days.

For dinner with Chad's biological parents Vicky dressed in the same long skirt and blouse she'd worn when Chad had taken her to the classy restaurant a few weeks ago. But she felt like a dowdy chicken compared to Lorene's elegance. Although Vicky had never bought designer clothes, she'd seen enough fashion shows to recognize them.

She was convinced that Lorene's white cashmere suit and blouse had been made by a New York designer. And the three strands of pearls and matching earrings hadn't come from a department store. Vicky wore the earrings Chad had given her, which flattered her ego a little.

While Vicky liked Chad's biological parents, it gave her some small comfort to realize that even the mistake they had made in conceiving Chad had turned out for good. But she felt intimidated in the Saunders's presence, much more than she had when she visited in the Reece household. Chad's adoptive parents were regular, everyday people, more like Vicky's family.

But she considered both Perry and Lorene superintelligent people, and of course Chad had inherited that same intelligence from both of them. Her lack of a college education embarrassed her and she found it impossible to join in the conversation around the table. She spent her time entertaining Amy.

Chad noticed her silence, and it troubled him. Didn't she like Perry and Lorene? He had been pleased during their visit to Alabama that Vicky and his mom and dad got along so well. But he wanted her to like his biological parents, too.

Lorene and Perry tried to draw her into their conversation, and Vicky was polite, but she was tense and nervous most of the time. Chad was dissatisfied with the evening as a whole. And he was hurt when she was always busy with Amy and didn't find time to say much to Perry and Lorene. His pleasure that they might settle in the Columbus area was dimmed by the fact that Vicky hadn't seemed to like them.

Perry and Lorene stayed only two days after the surgeon checked Perry and released him for biyearly visits with a specialist in California. The day before they left, Chad took them to see the residential sections of Columbus and its suburbs. But since their idea of relocating was in early stages, they had no idea where they would settle if they did move.

Chapter Thirteen

Cradling her phone in her hands, Vicky remembered the biblical patriarch's reconciliation with his brother Esau. Aloud she said, "Well, Jacob, I'm not sure how you had the courage to eat humble pie, but I'm going to find out if I can get up enough nerve to dial this phone."

The sudden ringing of the phone startled Vicky and the phone almost slid out of her hand. "Ironic!" she said, when she noted the caller. *How's that for timing, God!*

She let the phone ring five times before she pushed the talk button.

"Good morning, Mom!"

"Good morning to you, too," Rachel said. "Dad asked for biscuits and sausage gravy this morning. Why don't you come and join us?"

For a moment Vicky was tongue-tied.

"I'd love to do that. I intended to come to

see you this morning, but to get a good breakfast was more than I expected. I just finished dressing—I'll leave right away."

Rachel was taking a pan of from-scratch biscuits out of the oven when Vicky entered from the back porch. She sniffed appreciatively the aroma of fresh-baked bread. With a big apron wrapped around his waist, Steve lifted a steaming skillet from the stovetop and carried it to the table.

"Hi, Dad." Vicky kissed his cheek as he held a chair for her to sit down. This gesture that had once been commonplace earned Vicky an appraising glance from her mother.

"What do you want to drink?" Rachel asked.

"Green tea, if you have it. I read that green tea is good for my health—I'm trying it."

Rachel pulled out a chair and sat down. "Steve has an early appointment, so I'll get the tea as soon as we have grace." They joined hands while Steve prayed for God's blessings on the food.

If her father had to leave soon, Vicky realized that she couldn't delay her apology. She would not let this opportunity pass—her whole future could depend on it.

She halved two biscuits and spread them with several spoons of brown gravy filled with bits of sausage. She pulled the individual bowl of citrus fruit closer to her plate. She lifted a forkful of food to her lips and laid it back on her plate.

"This looks like a meal fit for a king but I can't eat until I say what I came here to say." Her eyes were downcast but she sensed her parents' surprise. Why did she find this so difficult to do?

After a long pause, during which she fought to still her trembling lips, Vicky said, "I apologize for the pain I've caused you during the past three years. I've been wrong, and I'm asking your forgiveness."

"But, Vicky," Steve said, and Vicky shook her head.

"Let me finish." Closing her eyes, she said, "I've been acting like a spoiled brat. I've made several wrong choices and I've had a long, pity party. It's over now. I want to start over with you and God."

Vicky opened her eyes to find her parents kneeling by her chair. They took her hands, and Steve lifted the one he held to his lips.

"Welcome home, daughter, and I know that God has welcomed you, too. We're not exactly guiltless in this situation. Maybe if we'd been better parents, you might have come to us sooner. We thought we knew what was best for you, forgetting that what we wanted might not be what you or God wanted."

Tears blinded Vicky's eyes and choked her voice.

Rachel took some tissues from the box on the cabinet and handed them to Vicky. "We won't interfere with your choices again. But don't shut us out of your life."

"I won't. I don't know what I want right now, except I'm convinced that God hasn't released me from the vow I made to serve Him. I took up His cross at the Belleville church. Since I've laid it aside, I want to go back to take it again. Will you go to services with me there next Sunday?"

"Of course, we will," Steve said. "I often think about our close fellowship with those people. There's a lot to be said for a small congregation."

Although there was a hint of tension between Chad and Vicky after Lorene and Perry left, they had kept in touch. After her reconciliation with her parents, Vicky called Chad.

She explained about her visit to her parents. "I'm planning to go to the church where I made my vow to Christian service. Mom and Dad are going with me. I'd like for you to be there, too."

"I wouldn't miss it," he said.

That Sunday, flanked by her parents and Chad, Vicky felt well armored when she entered the small sanctuary of Belleville Christian Church the following Sunday morning. The service hadn't started as yet, and many members of the congregation who remembered Vicky and her family greeted them warmly.

Mr. Lanham took Chad in hand and introduced him to everyone. Chad appreciated the fact that he didn't make any mention of Chad's career, but several people picked up on the name and mentioned his football games.

When they were seated, with Vicky between him and her mother, Chad surveyed the small room. The sanctuary probably wouldn't hold more than fifty people, and no more than thirty were in attendance. He tried to envision Vicky growing up in a small community like this. These people must have influenced the compassion for suffering people that had prompted her to dedicate herself to full-time Christian service. It had taken a lot of courage for her to go alone to work with the Red Cross during the flood in West Virginia.

The very fact that she was filled with love for others had made her vulnerable in the two unfortunate relationships she had had. He wondered, as he often had since Vicky had told him, if she was still in love with that

Damon guy. He squirmed uncomfortably at the thought, and Vicky looked at him quickly, seeming to sense that he was troubled about something. He smiled brightly at her.

Her deep compassion had also prompted her to give herself toward his personal emotional healing. He wouldn't have come this far without her help.

Throughout the opening exercises and the sermon, Vicky's slender hands unconsciously twisted together and several times her shoulder brushed against Chad's. She felt that she had disappointed her friends because she hadn't kept the vow she had made. Her body was tense and Chad prayed for God to give her the courage and the words that He would have her speak.

The minister closed his sermon with a prayer and stepped from the pulpit to announce the closing song. He gave an invitation to all who had a need to come forward for prayer.

The congregation sang the first verse. Vicky didn't move and Chad wondered if she had changed her mind.

During the singing of the second verse, however, she nodded to Chad and he stepped out into the aisle to let her walk by him. Her mother followed. Chad wondered if he should go with her, but he hesitated. This was Vicky's hour—he shouldn't intrude.

She talked briefly with the pastor and knelt at the altar with her mother and the pastor beside her. The congregation finished the remaining verses of the song and stood, with bowed heads, as the pianist continued to play softly.

At last, Vicky stood, and faced the assembly with a determination on her face that Chad had never seen before. There was a slight tremor in her voice, but as he watched her, Chad experienced a feeling for Vicky that was far from platonic. Vicky had made it plain from the first that she wasn't interested in romance. If he did love her, as he was beginning to suspect, and she didn't return his love, how could they continue their friendship?

"Many of you were here several years ago when I came forward in a service such as this and took up my cross submitting my life to full-time service to God. I'm ashamed to admit that while I kept that vision burning for a few years, in the stress of adulthood, I lost my enthusiasm. For the past few years I've been out of fellowship with God because I knew, in my heart, that I wasn't fulfilling the vow I'd made."

"Bless her, Lord," the pastor encouraged.

"A few weeks ago I promised that I would

take up my cross again and I came today for that purpose. I thought it was appropriate for me to renew my vow at the place where I'd first taken it. I've never known why God called me into His service for I don't have a lot to offer except a willing heart. But the words of the closing hymn today spoke to my heart, 'Though your talents may be few, give to God whatever you have, for what you give to Jesus He can multiply for you.'"

Accustomed to a more formal worship service than this one, Chad was touched that the entire congregation rushed forward to either hug Vicky or shake her hand. Chad eagerly waited his turn. Gathering her into his arms, he held her snugly. And since some others had greeted her with a kiss, Chad brushed his lips against her cheek. She stared up at him with a glint of wonder in her eyes as he moved on to make room for Steve to greet his daughter.

Joy surged through his heart as he realized what had happened to him. Despite his eagerness to tell Vicky how he felt, he knew he would have to bide his time. It would be a long time, if ever, before Vicky would be open to another relationship. When he contemplated the love that Vicky had showered on the other two men, he experienced a burning, angry sensation that he diagnosed as nothing except old-fashioned jealousy. Who would have thought that Chad Reece would stoop to that—to be jealous of two men he hadn't even met?

Vicky's face was radiant when they walked out of the church with her parents.

"Let's celebrate," Chad said. "I'd like to take you out to dinner."

"I have a better plan," Mrs. Lanham said. "I want you to come to the house for lunch."

Chad checked with Vicky and when she nodded that it was all right, he agreed.

The Lanhams lived in a two-story frame house in East Columbus which they had bought when Vicky was a teenager. Built in 1920, the house had been neglected and needed a lot of repair, but over a period of several years, Steve had transformed it into comfortable living quarters. The kitchen had been his first project and his efforts had resulted in a well-lit room with all the modern conveniences that Rachel wanted.

Chad and Steve watched a football game on television in the living room until Rachel mashed potatoes and took roast beef and vegetables from the oven. After dinner was over all four of them finished watching the NFL game and Chad had only a few uneasy moments when he realized anew that this part of his life had ended.

* * *

Chad had told Howie not to bother him during Perry and Lorene's visit, but the morning after they returned to California, the agent called.

"Is it a good time to talk, Chad?"

"Yes, and I have good news for you. I'm going to authorize the biography."

Howie's loud cheer nearly deafened Chad.

"I have a few stipulations, however."

Howie groaned. "Don't spoil it now."

"I'm not going to spoil anything. I simply want final approval on what they put in print. Add some kind of a clause in the contract that if they publish anything without my approval, they will be penalized. They can publish the truth, but I don't want a lot of nonsense included just to sell books. I'll leave the financial negotiations strictly up to you, but they have to meet with my approval, too."

"You're a hard taskmaster, buddy."

"I've let you get by with too much in the past, so it was time to pull on the reins."

The deal was signed with a generous advance, and Chad instructed his accountants to put this money in a special account separate from his other investments. All during the months of April and May, Chad worked with his agent, accountant and the editors, both in and out of Pittsburgh. He cleared out his apartment, planning to settle in Columbus permanently. On one of his trips to Pittsburgh, he had dinner with his former teammates without a twinge of regret that he wouldn't be playing with them again. This was the biggest test he'd had since the accident, and he called Vicky to tell her he had passed the test with flying colors.

The publisher sent editors to Alabama to interview the Reeces, to take pictures of the local sites that had been a part of Chad's life—his schools and the church he attended. His mother called to say that she had loaned the editor the scrapbooks that she had kept through the years.

During this same time Chad met another editor at his Pittsburgh apartment where video clips of all of his NFL games were stored. While he was there he gave up his apartment. His housekeeper packed all of his clothes and other possessions and he put them in storage to be eventually shipped to wherever he made his home.

One by one he was cutting ties with the past, and he actually looked forward to the publication of the book. He returned to Columbus still uncertain about what plans God had for his future.

* * *

The interview in Chicago was televised nationwide in mid-June and Vicky watched it with her parents, whom she visited more often now. Chad's personality and the strength of his character came through, and the viewers flooded the station with requests for more information about Chad. The publishers were overjoyed that his continued popularity assured the success of his biography when it hit the stands. The publisher had projected the first of August as the publication date and was already setting up book signings for Chad around the country.

"Strike while the iron is hot," Howie had advised. "Popularity doesn't last forever."

Because he was so busy with the editors, days would go by when Vicky and Chad didn't talk. When he had time, she was at work. When she was home in the evening, he was involved with reporters. Vicky accepted this—just as she had expected it would be, but she felt humiliated when she sensed that her parents were feeling sorry for her again.

By now Vicky knew that what she felt for Chad exceeded any emotion she had experienced in her previous relationships. She had healed from those unfortunate affairs, but she realized that there would be no ease for her heartbreak when Chad went out of her life.

She wouldn't have had it any other way. She still believed that God had brought them together for a reason. She took pride in knowing that if she hadn't been there for Chad, he might not have reached the height of popularity he was experiencing now.

But Chad missed her, and when he returned from an appointment with his New York publisher in late June, even though it was late at night, he called.

"Hope I didn't get you out of bed."

"I'm in bed, but reading. I had the phone nearby."

"It seems like ages since I've seen you. When do you have some free time?"

"I'm working all day tomorrow because the store manager is out of town, but I'm going to a special service at the church tomorrow night. A missionary from Haiti is going to speak. Why don't you come with me to that?"

"Will we have time for dinner first?"

"A quick one. I work until five and the meeting starts at seven. I'll walk to work in the morning and you can pick me up at the store. We can stop at a fast-food restaurant on our way to the church."

As they entered the church, they stopped to view pictures of the mission work in Haiti displayed in the church lobby. Ravages of a hurricane were evident in the small town where a church and orphanage were located.

The meeting was held in a chapel rather than the large sanctuary and the crowd was sparse. The missionary, Floyd Hobson, was an African-American and he and his family were on short-term leave in the States. He presented a PowerPoint summary of the work he was doing and spoke at length of the needs in the small village. Chief among the problems was the devastation of their house of worship by a hurricane the previous fall. The orphanage had been repaired until it could be used, but no funds were available for rebuilding the church. After the missionary finished his presentation, the church's pastor stood.

"Our church has supported this mission work for several years, and we asked Floyd to speak tonight. Our church board is sponsoring a mission group to go to Haiti in September to rebuild their church. Monetary contributions will be welcomed, but a work crew is needed. We have some volunteers, but we need more. Building skills aren't required because one of the premier building contractors in Columbus is sending two of his men to supervise the work. All you need are two hands and a willing heart. Talk to me after the benediction if you can answer this call." And seemingly as an afterthought, he said, "And you'll need some money to take care of your travel expenses."

Laughter from the audience greeted this important oversight.

Vicky and Chad exchanged glances. She smiled and nodded her head. Words weren't necessary to know that she, too, had taken the call personally, but he wondered if she could afford to pay her expenses. He took hold of her hand and squeezed it. The experience was such a strong one that he knew the call was from God. Of all the things he had expected God to call him to do, building a church on the island of Haiti was the last thing he would have imagined.

Chad continued to hold Vicky's hand as they exited the pew and started up the aisle toward the pulpit. He had his marching orders at last, and it felt great to be doing something. He'd been in limbo too long.

"We're interested in taking the mission trip," he said after they greeted the pastor and shook the missionary's hand.

"Great! Sign your names in the book," he said, indicating a notebook on a nearby table. "Can you come to an orientation meeting in the fellowship hall tomorrow night?"

"I can," Chad said, and Vicky added, "I'll be here."

As they drove home, they talked excitedly about the opportunity.

"I had the same feeling when he was talking as I did when I first felt my call to Christian service. I have no doubt that all of these years God has been preparing me for this moment."

"I'll pay your expenses," Chad said.

Vicky's glance in his direction wasn't friendly.

"No, thank you," she said coldly.

"I didn't intend to offend you," Chad said. "You said you didn't have the money for a plane trip to Alabama, so I don't see how you can afford a three-week missionary trip to Haiti. You'll even be missing your salary at the bookstore. I'd consider it part of my contribution to the project."

Vicky knew that she was being contrary, but now that her friendship for Chad had been complicated by love, she was hesitant to take anything from him.

"I appreciate your offer, but I wouldn't have volunteered for this trip if I couldn't pay for it. I must sacrifice *something* to do this. If you pay all of my expenses, then it will cost me nothing. I have a little nest egg that I've been harboring for several years. When my great aunt died she left me a legacy of four thousand dollars. That money has been in a savings account earning a little interest. I'll use that."

Hearing the finality in her voice, Chad said no more.

Chapter Fourteen

Chad picked Vicky up at six o'clock to go to the orientation meeting. He parked in front of the apartment complex and took the stairs to her apartment two at a time, marveling at how his stamina had increased since his surgery five months ago.

He tapped on the door and waited. "Chad?" she called.

"Yes."

"I'll be there in a second."

She opened the door. "I'm not quite ready. Come in for a minute."

He stepped inside the living area, which was divided from the kitchen by a serving bar. He felt as if he was in a closet. "The bedroom and adjoining bath are even smaller," she said, laughing at his expression.

"It's fine for you," he answered quickly, but

he had compared it to the elegant, spacious rooms he enjoyed everyday.

"You probably think I'm crazy for living here when I could be living with my folks and occupying a nice bedroom that's larger than this apartment."

"No, I don't think that," he assured her. "I know exactly how you feel. I lived with my folks through college, but I did that because it was less expensive and my company meant a lot to them. But I paid them back for all they'd spent on me and more when I set up a trust fund for their retirement. I understand your reason for living here."

She picked up her coat and he held it as she shrugged into it and zipped it.

"Are you excited?" she said as she preceded him down the narrow steps.

"Yes, I am. I've been singing most of the day, but it must not have been very melodious for Grace came upstairs in midafternoon, tapped on my door and asked me if I was sick."

Vicky joined his shout of laughter, and one of the tenants on the first floor stuck her head out of her door.

"What's going on?" she demanded, which only made Vicky and Chad laugh louder until the woman slammed the door on their merry-making.

Vicky slid into the front seat of his car when he opened the door.

"I know this trip isn't going to be any picnic, and I'll settle down to grim reality soon, but my prayers have been answered, in part, at least. I'm so thankful I can't stop rejoicing."

He buckled his seat belt and pulled out into the street.

"That's exactly how I've felt all day. I've been lost in a wilderness for three years, wandering around trying to find my way out. Suddenly, I've found a road that I can follow to go home. It's the same feeling I had when I volunteered to go with the Red Cross to help in the aftermath of the flood. I'm going to make a difference in the lives of other people—that's all I've ever wanted to do."

"I called my parents, as well as Perry and Lorene. Mom and Dad weren't sure it was the right thing for me to do, but as always, they accepted my decision. Perry and Lorene were as excited as we are. 'Humph' was Grace's only comment, but I'm convinced she's proud of me."

"My parents didn't turn a hair when I told them, and Dad even offered to pay my expenses."

Chad negotiated a left turn on Broad Street,

chuckling as he remembered a conversation with his agent.

"Howie just about hit the ceiling when he found out. Even though I told him not to, he's been negotiating other television and radio interviews for me. He had one scheduled for the time we'll be in Haiti to coincide with the beginning of the new season. I told him to cancel it and not reschedule without my permission. He wasn't very happy."

Floyd Hobson, the missionary, greeted them at the door and directed them to the conference room. Several people had already arrived and stood in small groups talking. Erica Long, whom Vicky had known for several years, called to them from the kitchenette at the back of the room.

"Come and have snacks and drinks before the meeting starts," she said. Erica stood behind a folding table holding several plates of deli cookies, a coffee server and several cans of soft drinks.

Chad and Vicky picked up cans of cola and put several cookies on one plate, which they would share. They moved to a round table near the podium, already occupied by a middle-aged couple.

The man reached his hand across the table to Chad. "I'm Smith Baxter," he said, "and this is my wife, Liz. We belong to a church in Cincinnati, but Reverend Hobson is a member of our church. When we knew he was taking this tour group we signed on."

"My name is Chad Reece and this is my friend, Vicky Lanham."

A speculative expression passed across Mr. Baxter's face when Chad introduced himself, as if the name sounded familiar, but he continued, "This is our second missionary trip. We went to Nicaragua once."

"My first," Chad said.

"This is the first outside the country for me," Vicky explained, "but I worked on a Red Cross disaster team once."

The missionary entered the room, followed by two men who were strangers to Vicky. Erica came and sat beside Vicky.

"If everyone will take a seat," Floyd said, "we'll get started. We have a lot to discuss. First of all, let's have prayer."

He spoke briefly, thanking God for those who had volunteered and asking His blessing on the work tour they were planning.

"This is a get-acquainted meeting as well as orientation," Floyd said. He indicated the two men who had entered the room with him. "Some of you may recognize Keith and Alvin Cross, who are among the major building contractors in this region. Although I value all of your participation, I especially appreciate these men for taking three weeks away from their business to help build a church.

"Contrary to what the general public may think, we aren't going on a vacation. The people of Haiti are the poorest in the Western Hemisphere, and in the village where we're going, our living conditions will be primitive. The weather is mild during this season of the year, and we'll sleep in tents on cots. It will be a challenge for our cooks to prepare food."

He lifted several folders. "Everyone should take one of these instruction folders and study them carefully so you'll know exactly what preparations you must make. Included is a list of personal things to take—medications and health items in particular. You must get a passport if you don't already have one. Instructions about obtaining passports are on the sheet, also, as well as the kind of clothing to take. In former missionary tours I've directed, after the participants see how poor the people of Haiti are, they leave most of their garments behind when we come home. So pack accordingly."

"We left everything except the clothes on our back in Nicaragua," Liz Baxter whispered.

"One thing we must always remember," the missionary continued, "is that while we're going to build a church, our most important mission is to build the Church of Christ. We are His representatives to the people we meet, many of whom do not know Him."

Vicky had brought a notebook along and she made notes on things they must remember. Each volunteer was asked to pay two thousand dollars which would take care of the plane fare, their food in Haiti, most of which would be bought in the United States and taken with them, and hotel accommodations in Port-au-Prince on their arrival and departure.

After he finished his explanation, Reverend Hobson asked each volunteer to mention what area of expertise they could contribute to the missionary project. "And since we'll experience a lot of close communion in the next month or so, we might as well get on a first name basis to start with. Just call me Floyd."

Most of the men had some kind of experience that would be helpful in construction—an electrician, a plumber, a painter. Smith Baxter said that he and his wife had no construction skills to contribute, but they wanted to provide Bible classes for adults or children during the two weeks they were in the village.

Chad and Vicky exchanged helpless glances. In his excitement of believing that God meant for him to go to Haiti, he hadn't considered what he could do when he got there. From Vicky's defeated expression, he knew that she, too, hadn't gotten beyond the excitement of going to the mission field at last.

Erica Long, a plump, matronly woman, smiled widely, "I've done a lot of painting in my own house, and I can do that if needed, but I guess somebody will have to prepare food for the mission team. I'm a pretty good cook, if I do say so, and I'll try to keep food on the table."

Chad and Vicky were the only ones who hadn't spoken, and he motioned for her to go ahead.

"I don't have any skills—I'm not even an experienced cook, but I felt God's call to go. There ought to be something I can do."

"You can help me, Vicky," Erica said.

"Let me interrupt a moment," the missionary said. "We don't expect our volunteers to be skilled workers. A willing heart is probably the best asset anyone can have. I fully believe that it's God's will for this group to go to Haiti as a team, and He can use any talents you have."

Chad unfolded his tall frame and Vicky's heart seemed to turn a somersault. What a man! Handsome as the dawn, and unpretentious as a newborn with the personality of a beloved pet. How could she be fortunate enough to be his friend? Better a friend than nothing, she thought, and hoped that she could conceal her feelings from Chad. When they were going to be together almost constantly for three weeks in Haiti, it would be hard to do.

Vicky could tell he had the group captivated before he said a word. After giving his name, he said, "Like Vicky, I don't know the first thing about construction. I know the difference between a hammer and a saw, but not how to use either one. But when Floyd made his appeal for helpers, I felt the same urge that Isaiah must have felt when he saw the Lord high and lifted up in the temple. I didn't hear the doorposts and thresholds shaking and the sanctuary wasn't filled with smoke, as it was in the prophet's vision, but the voice of God spoke to my heart. I knew right away the message was meant for me. That's all I have to offer, but I believe it will be enough."

"I believe it will be, too, Chad," the missionary said tenderly.

One of the contractors, Keith Cross, had turned to stare at Chad when he gave his name. When Chad sat down, Keith laughed and said, "I'm afraid Chad is hiding his light under a bushel. He might not know much about building construction, but I'd trade my craft any day to be able to play football like he can."

Everyone in the room focused on Chad.

Vicky wondered how much it cost him to say evenly, "Make that in the past tense—like I *could*. If you recognize me, you probably also know that I won't be playing football anymore."

"Yes," Keith answered. "I saw your television interview last week. A bad break, Chad."

"Two months ago, I couldn't talk about it and would have agreed with you. But I'm convinced that everything has happened in my life for a reason. As long as God is leading the way, I'll be all right."

The assembled group clapped their hands in agreement.

"We have a diverse group of volunteers," Floyd said, "and we bring a lot of talent and experience to this project. Lumber, nails, roofing and other supplies needed to build the church have already been shipped and hopefully they will be there before we are. What we need to do tonight is start listing what we want to take with us. Let's think about food first, and since we'll be taking it with us, think light. We can buy fresh vegetables and fruit in markets in the cities, as well as other food items, but Haitian diets are different from ours. We'll do well to take what we can."

"Since we've been to Nicaragua, we have some ideas, Liz Baxter said. "Take cake mixes that don't need eggs."

"Who will write down the list as we go along?"

Vicky held up her hand and flipped a page in her notebook.

"See, Vicky," Floyd said, "you've found a job already."

The other two women and some men who cooked suggested dried beans, instant potatoes, dried soup, boxes of puddings, biscuit mix and pancake mix until Vicky had a sizable list.

"We will think of more things later. Some of you may think we're making plans too far in advance, but the next two months will pass quickly, because there are many preparations to make," Floyd said. "Now we will need a treasurer— someone to keep track of our funds. Since not many people feel like volunteering to handle other people's funds, I'm going to ask Smith Baxter to take care of that. Before you leave, if all of you will give Smith the fee, he can have the church treasurer hold the money until we're ready to go. Either a check or cash will do. Those of you buying the foodstuffs will have to withdraw some of that money soon. The balance can be taken in traveler's checks."

Chad had gotten enough cash to pay his fee, but Vicky wrote a check for the amount.

"I'll help Erica put away the food and wash the coffee cups," she said. "It won't take long."

"I'm in no hurry."

Chad picked up two information kits and sat at one of the tables. While he waited for Vicky he opened the packet to read their itinerary and instructions. Keith Cross came to sit beside him.

"I should have kept my mouth shut, Chad. Maybe you'd just as soon no one knew of your NFL career."

"It's okay. I spent several miserable weeks dodging people, thinking my life was over. I was mad at myself, mad at God, just a regular pain in the neck to everyone, especially my family. But I'm all right now. I really am!" he insisted when he saw doubt in Keith's eyes. "Fame fades about as fast as it comes, so within a few years, my football career will be forgotten." He smiled kindly.

"Does anyone want any more coffee before we throw it away?" Erica called.

"I could handle another cup," Keith said. "How about you, Chad?"

"No coffee, but I'll drink another can of diet pop."

They joined Vicky and Erica, who were discussing their cooking assignment.

"I'll buy a book of Haitian recipes," Erica

said. "I'm not going to live for three weeks in a foreign country and live on macaroni and cheese out of a box." She made a face. "There are some Haitian restaurants in Columbus, and I might take dinner there some evening. If I can find some interesting foods, we can take some of those ingredients with us, too."

Vicky gave Erica her phone number. "Call me and we can get together and plan some of the meals before we go shopping."

Vicky's boss wasn't happy about her three weeks' absence during one of the store's busiest times and she fired her. Vicky volunteered to finish the week to give the manager time to find a replacement. She didn't tell her parents or Chad about the situation, but she did talk to God about it. The only answer she received was to go back to college and prepare to follow her dream.

The next day she went to the OSU registrar's office, discussed student loans and registered for the winter semester. In the meantime, she had to have an income.

"God," she prayed silently, when she entered the business office, "I need a job. I'll take anything that's available."

She talked to the director of volunteer services first, a prim elderly woman who had been a Biology professor before she retired. Vicky explained about the missionary tour and that she had been fired.

"I'll be starting classes next quarter, but I need a job before then. And I'll have to continue working while I'm studying."

"You've been one of our best volunteers," the director said, "and I'll go to bat for you. If at all possible, you'll have a job as soon as you come home from Haiti. You're being faithful to God's call, and He never leaves faithful followers out on a limb. One way or another He always provides."

After she left the hospital, Vicky went to see her parents, rather than taking the coward's way out and telling them on the phone.

"Vicky!" her mother cried. "Why didn't you tell us? You know we put aside money for your college education. We'll pay your tuition and you can move back home to live. Your room is just as you left it—waiting for you to come home."

Tears stung Vicky's eyes. It was comforting to have good rapport with her parents again.

"It may come to that," she said, "but let me try it on my own first."

"Have you settled on a major?" her father asked.

"No. I signed up for twelve hours of basic,

required subjects. After so many months away from college I'll have to ease into studying."

"Have you considered that this trip to Haiti may impact what kind of vocation you pursue?" he said.

"Yes, I expect it to, but I couldn't wait until I returned from there before I made some provision for the next few months."

"Promise me something," her mother said. "We aren't going to meddle in your decisions, but will you please come to us if you need financial help?"

"Yes, that I will promise. I just pray it won't be necessary."

Her phone rang before she got back to the apartment. She signaled, turned toward the curb and stopped before she answered.

"Vicky, this is Chad. I bought two Creole dictionaries today, which will help us communicate with the Haitians. If you aren't working tonight, can you come by so we can study some of the common phrases? I'll order in lasagna and salads."

"Yes, I'd like to do that."

"What time is good for you?"

"I can be there by half past six."

"I'll ask Grace to eat with us, too. She brought up a peach pie this afternoon."

"Looks like everyone else is contributing something. What can I bring?"

"An appetite."

"That sounds like a good arrangement," Vicky answered humorously, deciding to wait until later to tell Chad she didn't have a job.

Chapter Fifteen

Grace insisted on washing the dishes and tidying up the kitchen so Vicky and Chad could start their language lessons. Chad didn't argue because Grace didn't approve of his housekeeping methods. They moved everything off of the table to the sink cabinet. Vicky wiped the tabletop with a damp cloth and dried it and they sat side by side. He gave her one of the dictionaries and he opened the other.

Vicky slid a pen and notebook close to her right arm.

"I had two years of French in high school and I think the Creole pronunciation is similar." She flipped through the small book. "Most of these words are spelled almost like French but not quite. For instance, hello or good morning in French is *bonjour*. In Creole they drop the *r*."

"I studied Spanish in high school and German in college, but I don't have any French. You'll have to help me."

Vicky flipped through the book. "This is a good dictionary. The pronunciation symbols are easy to follow. As long as we keep these books with us, we can find our way around in Haiti."

"And of course Floyd can speak both English and Creole. We can always rely on him. But I still want to be prepared for the times Floyd isn't with us."

"Let's each pick five words or phrases that we think are most essential and focus on them tonight."

"Okay, I'll go first," Chad said. "I'll start with *okay* because I use it a lot. *Oke* is okay. *Wi* is Yes. *Mesi* is thanks. *Non* is no. *Eskize nwen* means excuse me. Nothing hard about this!"

"Maybe, but the Haitians might not understand us. I'll choose some questions that we may need. *Mwen malad* means I'm sick. *Eske ou ka ede nou, souple?* is translated 'Can you help us, please?' We'll probably use that phrase often."

Grace finished the dishes and sat down at the table listening to them.

"Humph. You'd better find out how to say, 'do you speak English?'" she commented.

"A good idea," Vicky agreed. "Here it is.

Eske ou pale angle? And since Erica and I will be buying food items, we'd better learn to say, *Konben?* That's 'how much?' or 'how many?' *Eske ou gen?* means 'do you have?'" Vicky giggled. "Here's a good one—*Kote nou ye?*"

"Let's see if I can figure it out. I studied the words for an hour or so this afternoon. It must be something you think we need to know. I've got it! 'Where are we?'"

"Good. Now let me find one more. Just in case some of us get sick, we could use this, *Kote lopital la?*"

"Where is the hospital?" Grace said and Vicky and Chad clapped their hands.

"Maybe you'd better go with us," Chad said. "We could use another cook."

"Nope! Downtown Columbus is far enough away from home for me."

That comment made Chad wonder if he would be successful in his plan to buy the house from Grace, who stood up and started toward the door.

"I won't interfere with your lessons any longer," she said. "I'm going downstairs now. Thanks for supper."

They worked for another hour before Chad pushed back from the table. "My mind has taken all it can for one night."

"But we've learned a lot."

"Enough to find our way around the country if we have to. Let's rest awhile. How about some ginger ale?"

"I'd like that," Vicky said as she stood and stretched. "I've been sitting too long—my legs and back are stiff."

She shuffled into the living room and went through a series of leg stretches while Chad put ice into two glasses and poured ginger ale from a two-liter bottle.

When he joined her, she took a long drink from the glass. "I lost my job today."

He stared at her, an incredulous expression in his eyes. "What?"

"My boss wouldn't give me permission to leave for three weeks, so she fired me. I'll work a week until she finds someone to replace me."

"That's quite a sacrifice to make to go on this trip, isn't it?"

She shrugged her shoulders and sat on the couch. "Not really. It isn't a rewarding job." She continued to tell him about her day—enrolling for classes at OSU, getting a promise of a job at the hospital and of her parents' approval of her plans.

"I feel good about the whole situation, especially the response from Mom and Dad. It's good to know I can go back home to live if I have to, but I hope it won't come to that."

Chad knew that he was assuming a lot and heading off on a tangent in his dreams, but for the past few days he kept thinking of buying Grace's home and bringing Vicky here as his bride. Not once had he seen any indication from Vicky that she considered him any more than a friend, so was he just building disappointment for himself to even consider such a scenario? Was it possible that her unfortunate romances, especially the last one with Damon, had left her without any desire for love?

Remembering their instruction from Floyd, Chad and Vicky planned to be at the Columbus International Airport three hours before their departure to Haiti. Because of the large amount of items the mission group was taking, they had to be at the airport earlier than most passengers.

Vicky's parents volunteered to bring her to the airport, and to Chad's surprise, Grace insisted that she would drive him. Her car was ten years old, but he sneaked a peek at the odometer and saw that the mileage was only ten thousand. As he might have expected, she was a careful, competent driver, but she didn't want to park in the airport garage, so she left him at the loading level.

She unlocked the trunk and he motioned for

the skycap to unload his luggage to take into the terminal. He had loaded it into Grace's car, but Chad wanted to be as cautious as possible. He was cognizant of the fact that Haiti wasn't the best place in the world for him to have a relapse of some kind so he intended to accept help when possible.

"Chad, you be careful," Grace said, and he was startled to see tears in her eyes.

"Don't worry Grace. I'll be back in three weeks—no doubt a wiser man than I am now." He reassured her.

"I'm just a foolish old woman. Don't pay any attention to me. I always wanted a son and I guess I've sort of adopted you in my mind. I should have known better."

Chad put down his bag and pulled her into a bear hug. "I've got more parents now than any man should have, so one more won't matter. In this case, I'll adopt you instead of the other way around."

"Well, this is a touching scene," a man said and Chad looked up to see Steve Lanham watching him with a broad smile on his face.

"Hi, Steve. Meet my third mom. This is Grace Lashley, my landlady. Grace, this is Vicky's father."

Grace swiped away her tears and shook hands with Steve.

"Vicky has mentioned you," Steve said. "We got here a short time ago, and I took our car to the garage. Need any help?"

"No, the skycap is waiting to take in my luggage, so I'd better go. Don't worry about us, Grace."

Chad and Steve waved Grace on her way before they went inside the terminal.

"I couldn't have found a better place to live," Chad said. "She's a wonderful person."

While they waited for their departure time in the crowded waiting area, Chad and Vicky were seated apart from their fellow travelers. This gave Chad the opportunity to tell Vicky about his conversation with Grace.

"I hoped I'd have a private moment with you," he said. "Grace insisted on preparing my breakfast this morning. It was her contention that I wouldn't have another decent meal until we got back from Haiti."

"Obviously she doesn't have much confidence in Erica's and my cooking abilities."

His mouth twitched with amusement. "I hadn't thought about it that way."

"But she's probably right," Vicky said, grimacing in good humor.

"I've been praying about my idea of buying her house, but the time has never seemed right to broach the subject. But while we were eating, I felt encouraged to mention it."

She regarded him with somber curiosity. "You're sure that's what you want to do?"

"I'm sure. A lot of my future is still up for grabs, but I *am* sure that I want the house. And the strangest thing, I don't think she was surprised. It almost seemed that she *expected* me to make the offer."

"So she didn't turn you down?"

"No. But she didn't say she would sell to me, either. She quizzed me unmercifully during our drive to the airport. She wanted to know if I intended to *live* in the house or just dodge in once in a while. Did I intend to get married, settle down and have a family? I got the feeling that if I didn't answer yes to that last question she wouldn't sell to me."

Vicky lowered her thick lashes. She sensed that Chad was watching her. Her heart was hammering in her ears and her stomach clenched tight but she must not let him see how his words had shocked her. Her courage and determination were like a rock inside her—she would *not* allow him to see into the depths of her heart. She looked up at him with an effort, forcing a smile as she chose her words carefully.

"Well! If you don't show up with a bride

in tow, you might as well forget about buying Grace's house, huh?"

Even the thought tore at her insides. The day Chad Reece brought a bride to Columbus would be the day Vicky left Ohio forever.

Her comment hadn't told Chad anything about Vicky's feelings for him. But it sounded as if the thought didn't bother her at all. He was uncomfortable with his inability to figure her out.

"Yeah, it does seem that way. I will probably have to sign a contract of what I can and can't do with the house, but I'm confident that it will become my home."

"That's nice," Vicky said in a quiet voice, which told Chad nothing at all of her feelings for him. He sighed inwardly.

"Do you realize what today is?" he asked.

Surprised, Vicky said, "I'm not sure what you mean."

"It was one year ago that I had my accident."

"Oh, I know we've known each other for over a year, but I didn't remember the exact day of your injury."

With a faraway look in his eyes, Chad said, "Yes, a year ago today, and do you know, when I flew to Pittsburgh for the first game of the season last weekend, I sat in the bleachers and cheered as loud as I could. It didn't bother me at all that I wasn't playing. I knew then that I was healed. I have my new mission in life, and I'm thankful that God gave me two years of pro ball experience which netted enough money so that I could help others."

"That's wonderful news." Vicky took his left hand and held it to her lips.

Erica and the Baxters joined them. Chad's dark eyes flashed with tenderness and longing, as they turned to their new friends and focused on the mission to Haiti.

Two hours later the plane departed from the airport. Chad and Vicky had seats together and remembering how excited she was when she looked out the window on their way to Alabama, he insisted that she take the window seat. In Miami they loaded into a smaller plane that would take them to the airport at Port-au-Prince.

Vicky had her first view of the Atlantic from the air. And except for a few trips to Canada this was also Chad's first trip outside of the Continental United States so he was excited about crossing the nation's boundaries. Because the flight was a short one, the plane didn't reach a high altitude, and as the sky was cloudless, they were able to see the ocean throughout the flight. When the pilot hovered over Port-au-

Prince for a landing, Vicky saw palm trees, the surf beating against the beaches and numerous sailboats in a marina.

"This looks like Paradise—what I've always thought Hawaii looked like."

"Would you like to visit Hawaii?"

"Well, of course, but that's just another dream I never expect to come true." As the landing gear was released and the plane dropped closer to the ground, she recalled what Floyd Hobson had told them about the political and social situation in Haiti.

"It's hard to imagine that such a lovely place could be filled with crime, corruption, poverty and illness."

After their year's acquaintance Chad was well aware of Vicky's compassionate nature, and he understood how the situation distressed her. "But we're here to do what we can to alleviate those problems. It may not be much, but we're trying."

Vicky and Erica shared a room in the La Plaza Hotel for their overnight stay in Port-au-Prince. Chad roomed with Brian Estep, an electrician who had retired the previous year.

After they unpacked what they would need for overnight, Erica said, "I suspect this is going to be the last time we'll have a decent bath for two weeks, so let's take advantage of that nice pool downstairs before we dress for dinner."

The next morning, Chad and Vicky joined the rest of their group as they loaded into a red tourist bus to see highlights of the city. Chad knew little about Haiti, and he listened intently as the guide explained the history of the city in creditable English.

"The explorer Columbus visited our country on his first voyage to the New World in 1492 and claimed it for Spain. France established a colony here in the early seventeenth century and Spain eventually ceded the western part of the island to the French. In 1804 the inhabitants declared independence."

Although the tour bus took them to the city's best sites, Vicky couldn't overlook the obvious evidences of poverty everywhere. The bus stopped in one section and they walked among the people. The streets, buses and stores were overcrowded. And while prices on goods seemed low to her, she knew that they were beyond the means of most Haitians. And it was sad to know that government mismanagement and graft was probably the greatest cause of this poverty.

Floyd took Vicky and Erica to the marketplace where they bought some fruit, bread and other products they hadn't brought from the States. When Vicky commented on the crowded market, the missionary explained, "Residents of Haiti live from day to day. They don't have the privilege of going to one store where they can lay in supplies for a week."

Vicky was restless most of the night, irritated because she couldn't sleep. Not wanting to disturb Erica, she wrapped in a robe and stepped out on the balcony.

She couldn't put her finger on the cause of her restlessness. She was excited, and somewhat edgy, about their missionary project, but it was more than that. She sensed a difference in Chad. Was she imagining things or was he treating her more tenderly than he had? And she was hard put to understand some of the glances she intercepted when she caught him looking at her. Was he, too, starting to think that their relationship had developed into more than friendship, or was that just wishful thinking on her part?

Sometimes it was more than Vicky could bear. Hadn't she learned anything from her former experiences? But what could she do about it? She had been so confident that she would never love again. *Was* it love this time? None of the emotions she had felt about Damon came near to the overpowering love she had for Chad. She was ashamed to realize that her attraction for Damon was primarily physical, perhaps a natural reaction when her heart was already wounded. She was attracted to Chad physically, but it was much more encompassing—it was her life.

Sizing up the twenty-passenger bus waiting at the entrance to the hotel the next morning to take them to the village, Keith Cross said to Chad, "Must be at least fifteen years old."

"But it's probably the best available," Chad answered. "I'm a little surprised, though, for the sightseeing bus was modern."

"Putting their best foot forward for tourists," Keith answered. "I just hope this one holds up until we get to our destination."

The driver came to load their luggage on top of the bus, and everyone picked up their boxes and bags and handed them up to him. He tied ropes around the luggage and put the overflow on the rear seats of the bus.

With a skeptical look at the loaded bus, Vicky said, "Let's hope we don't lose a lot of it."

Chad followed her up the steps of the bus and ducked for the low door, but he didn't duck low enough.

"Ouch!"

Vicky turned. "Did you hurt yourself?"

"Not much, but if the rest of the bus is as solid as this doorway, we've got a good vehicle. It's a good thing I had on my OSU cap over a thick head of hair."

The missionary followed the bus in his station wagon and Smith and Liz Baxter rode with him. The seats were narrow so each of the passengers took a seat by themselves. Vicky sat right behind the driver and Chad chose the seat behind her.

After the business district of Port-au-Prince was behind them, Chad thought they were now seeing the real Haiti, not what tourists to the seaports were shown. Homes and businesses alike were in deplorable condition—worse than any slum area Chad had ever seen in the United States. Farmers worked their small acreages with mules or dilapidated tractors. Skinny, large-eyed children played around small ramshackle huts.

Chad reasoned that if God wanted him to find an outlet for his philanthropic projects, he had come to the right place. From the looks of things he could spend his entire fortune in Haiti and not make a dent in the poverty. About all he could do during this trip was to assess the needs and go from there. Without going through the proper channels anything he sent to Haiti could be confiscated by corrupt officials and the people still wouldn't be helped. He had to move slowly.

A few miles from Port-au-Prince the pavement ended, and the road that had once been covered with gravel was full of potholes, so numerous that the bus couldn't miss all of them. The driver's efforts to find smooth driving resulted in the bus swaying back and forth continually. Vicky grabbed the metal rail that separated her from the driver's seat and cast an amused glance over her shoulder.

The bus was top-heavy with all of their supplies and luggage. Chad rolled his eyes toward the roof of the bus.

"We'd better pray that those ropes hold or our things will be scattered."

"We'll have to go hungry if that happens. But the people who find the food might benefit."

"They might if they can read English and know how to prepare the food. According to Floyd, not many of these people can speak English."

Chad was convinced that this mission tour would teach him lessons he would never forget.

Chapter Sixteen

Floyd had told them earlier that Peti Ville had about two hundred inhabitants, plus the thirty children who lived in the orphanage. When the bus ground to a halt beside the hurricane-ravaged church, Vicky decided that the entire population must have been on hand to welcome them.

Children with outstretched hands crowded around the Americans as they stepped off the bus. Vicky could hardly restrain from emptying her pockets into those needy hands. Floyd had warned them, however, that they couldn't give to everyone. If they contributed to the community as a whole, they would reach more people than if they gave to the more aggressive individuals.

The pastor of the church, Pierre, a young man of slender stature greeted them in broken

English and welcomed them to his village. He pointed with pride to the tents prepared for the visitors. The doors of the tents stood open revealing narrow cots and Vicky wondered what sleeping on one of them would do to Chad's injury.

She noticed that there were two tents—one for the men, one for the women. Since there were only four women, they would be less crowded than the ten men.

Erica deposited her bags in the tent that Floyd indicated. "The first thing I want to see is where we'll be cooking," she muttered to Floyd.

He spoke to the pastor in Creole. Bowing, with his mouth parted in a broad smile that showed his white teeth, Pierre pointed toward a crude building beside the damaged church. *"La!"*

Vicky and Erica walked beside Floyd and the pastor to the building. Pierre motioned them to enter. Erica stopped abruptly on the threshold and threw a startled glance toward Vicky, who crowded around her and went inside the small room. The pastor pulled a string to turn on the light—a single, low-wattage bulb hanging from the low ceiling.

Vicky's head was only a couple of inches from the ceiling, and most of the male volunteers were taller than she was. "I don't believe we'll get any help from the guys in this kitchen," she said wryly.

Erica, still speechless, stepped into the room. Vicky assessed the equipment on which they had to provide three meals a day for fourteen people and any Haitians who invited themselves to dinner.

A sink with a cold water faucet stood in one corner. The ancient electric stove had four burners with an oven beneath the burners. A table stood to one side and several cabinets were built along one wall. One thing in the kitchen's favor—the room was spotlessly clean. The pastor, still smiling, watched Vicky and Erica expectantly.

Vicky forced a smile and nodded her head. They had provided the best they had—probably better equipment than anyone else in the village owned. She said to Floyd, "Tell him it is very nice and thank him for it."

Floyd spoke rapidly in Creole. Pierre bowed and his smile widened.

Finally coming out of her shock, Erica said, "Ask him how long the electricity is on each day. I understand many small towns don't have power all of the time."

"I can answer that," Floyd said. "The power plant is privately owned and the power is off from eleven o'clock until six the next morning. I hope you brought flashlights and plenty of bulbs."

"That was on our list of necessities," Erica said pertly. "But we can't cook with flashlights."

"You'll be surprised to learn what you can do when necessary," Floyd said, and he smiled, evidently amused at their discomfiture and shock. "I've hosted several work groups in Haiti and some of the volunteers' methods are ingenious."

Vicky looked at her watch. "It's an hour until lunchtime. Any suggestions for food?"

Erica seemed to have recovered from her initial shock and she answered confidently, "We can manage. Let's mix up a container of orange juice, open some jars of cheese spread and a box of crackers. We can serve the bananas we bought in Port-au-Prince last night with cookies. That will have to do."

"Sounds like a banquet to me," Floyd said.

"We'll have something hot for supper," Erica promised.

Chad stuck his head in the doorway. "Where do you want us to store these cartons?"

"There's a built-in wall cabinet that will hold quite a few items. But you'll bump your head if you come inside," Vicky said. "You men can bring the supplies to the door and we'll find a place for them."

A dozen or so children followed the Americans back and forth as they unloaded their possessions and stored them in the tents and the cookhouse.

"I put your bags in the tent," Chad told Vicky when he brought a box of food. "Floyd doesn't believe the natives will steal anything, but they are very curious. Be sure you lock up any valuables."

"I have my traveler's checks, money and passport in a security belt around my waist," Vicky said. "I didn't bring anything else of value."

"I didn't, either," Erica said. "Chad, look in here and see what we have to work with."

He ducked his head and came inside, careful not to stand upright.

"Keith and his brother are already making two long trestle tables and some benches for us to sit on when we have our meals. So they can no doubt build some temporary tables for you. And the electrician might be able to hook up a hot plate for extra cooking if there's one available."

"We labeled all of the boxes," Vicky said, "so if you haven't already, bring the cartons with cheese spread and crackers and the disposable plates and cups. When are you starting on the building?"

"This afternoon. Floyd and the Cross brothers are talking with the pastor now to find out what kind of building they need."

"We'll have lunch ready soon and will also fix something for an afternoon snack. We'll be better organized tomorrow."

When Floyd came to see how Erica and Vicky were getting along, he said, "You're welcome to use my station wagon any time you want to go to the market."

"I don't welcome many trips to Port-au-Prince over that rough road," Erica said.

"You don't have to go to Port-au-Prince. Saint-Marc is a seaport town, much closer, and the road is better. It's a good place to shop."

Erica and Vicky agreed that they could manage for the rest of the day, but would plan a shopping trip the next morning.

When twenty-five native children and adults stood watching when Vicky and Erica carried the food to the table, Floyd invited them to sit with the Americans.

"We must feed them, too," he said. "These people are curious more than hungry because the church leaders look after them, but we can't ignore them."

"I know," Vicky said. "We prepared extra

food. I couldn't eat if they didn't have anything."

After lunch was over, the Baxters drew the children aside and sat down with them to keep them out of the adults' way. Smith held up pictures while Liz read to them in English, and as Vicky passed by, she noticed that the children had learned a few English words.

"Let's make some brownies to see how the oven works," Erica suggested. "I'd rather experiment on cookies than an expensive dish of some kind."

It took the brownies twice as long to bake as the recipe on the box suggested but they were ready when the work crew needed a break. Erica had also heated a kettle of water on the stove and made instant coffee. If the food wasn't of the quality they were accustomed to, no one complained. Vicky suspected that by the time the project was finished there would be many complaints, but everyone was in a positive mood now about their mission tour. A quick camaraderie had formed between Chad and Pierre, and the pastor sat beside him as they ate. Vicky was amused when she heard Chad's feeble efforts to converse with Pierre in Creole.

By the time they sat down to their evening meal of tuna and noodle casserole, canned fruit and the rest of the brownies, Vicky realized that she had only been off her feet during the half hour they had eaten lunch. The natives had gone to their homes for the night because the Americans ate alone. Everyone gave a hand in cleaning the table and washing the plastic dishes they'd brought.

"You'll probably want to go to bed early tonight," Floyd said, "so let's have a short devotional period and then we can be on our own until morning. I'll read only one verse of Scripture which defines our purpose in being here. You will find this in the twenty-fifth chapter of Matthew, verse forty.

"The King will reply, 'I tell you the truth, whatever you did for one of the least of these brothers of mine, you did for me.'

"Your willingness to accept this command of our Lord has already blessed me. You've mastered the first hurdle—coming face-to-face with the terrific need of these people and your acceptance of the uncomfortable living conditions. I pray that your stamina and faith will sustain you through our days together. Let's bow in a moment of silent prayer as each of us shares the desires of our hearts with God."

In the distance Vicky could hear waves lapping against the shore. A gentle breeze sighed over their heads. Darkness was fast approaching.

God, you know my heart and that I want to serve You in some special way. Direct my thoughts and decisions. Amen.

When Floyd finished, Chad asked him, "Is there any reason we can't go to the beach?"

"It's safe enough, if that's what you mean. It's a nice little beach and only a short walk, but there won't be any lights so take one with you."

Vicky and Erica were discussing the breakfast menu when Chad joined them.

"I'm walking down to the beach. Do either of you want to go along?"

"Not me," Erica said. "I intend to go to bed as soon as possible."

"I'll go, but not for long," Vicky said.

They took the path Floyd had indicated. After a short walk, they climbed a sand dune and the sea lay before them. In the semidarkness the water seemed murky but the tide was coming in and white waves slapped the surface of the water in rhythmic motion.

Vicky breathed deeply. "Peaceful, isn't it? I needed a refresher. I didn't realize when God called me to take this mission trip that I'd start out as a cook. We've had a hard afternoon."

They sat on the warm sand of the dune.

Chad's strong left arm circled her waist. Taking a deep, unsteady breath, Vicky leaned against him. She drew strength from the power of his well-muscled body.

"There isn't any place on earth I'd rather be than here with you ready to begin the adventure of our lives. My anticipation of what's ahead for me, for *us*," he amended, "is more intense than when I was drafted for the NFL. It's strange how our priorities can shift in such a short time."

"I feel the same way, as if we've been anointed for this work." She laughed lightly. "I'm not sure I felt that way when Erica and I finally finished cooking for the day."

"The meals have been good, though."

"Anything tastes good when you're hungry," she said jokingly.

Chad's arm tightened and she snuggled closer, ignoring her conscience that kept trying to convince her she was making a mistake. *Remember your mother said that you don't have any common sense about men. Remember what it felt like when Damon, who seemed the answer to all you wanted in a man, walked off and left you. Remember your vow to never get close to another man.*

Vicky tried to recall all of those things, but as usual, her heart and her mind were in conflict. Paul the apostle said, "When I want to do good, evil is right there with me." But was there anything bad about her feelings for Chad? No! Her thoughts about any relationship with him were genuine. She didn't suppose he would ever feel about her as she did about him, but at least, in spite of her mother's accusation and her youthful emotions, she had a pure body to offer any man she chose to marry.

Although wanting to prolong this moment with Vicky obviously content in his arms, the waves were coming closer while the wind splayed moisture around them. Chad knew they both needed to rest.

He squeezed her waist and stood, lifting her upward with him. Darkness had surrounded them, and he couldn't see her expression. Before he released her, he murmured, "Is it all right if I kiss you?"

Her nerves tensed immediately and Chad feared he had made the wrong move. But she didn't pull away and slowly her body relaxed.

"Yes. I want you to kiss me," she said in a semiaudible voice.

His arms encircled her and she felt his uneven breathing on her cheek as he groped in the darkness for her lips. Turning toward him, she gave herself freely to his gentle kiss as soft as a whisper, drinking in the sweetness of his caress.

Chad had never given any girl more than a casual kiss, and the warmth of Vicky's lips sent spirals of delight through his veins. But he didn't want to push Vicky too far. He lifted his head and kissed the tip of her nose and released her.

Arms encircling each other's waist, in silence they returned to their campsite. Chad held a flashlight in his left hand to illuminate their way. Love had come to him at last! But he had to restrain his feelings until he knew how Vicky felt about him. Platonic friendship with Vicky now seemed as dull as a cold baked potato.

Both of the tents were still lighted and lively talk indicated that the volunteers hadn't yet gone to bed.

"Good night," Vicky said as they separated to go to their respective tents. She hoped her face didn't mirror the bubbling joy in her heart.

"Try to rest. Tomorrow will be a difficult day."

Vicky's response to his caress had stimulated his emotions to fever pitch. He doubted very much that he would take his own advice while he considered what the future held for Vicky and him.

* * *

The next evening when they sat down for their evening meal it seemed to Vicky that she had been in Haiti forever. Her life in Ohio was only a dream of the past. The weariness of her companions as they grouped around the table was amusing but also heart-wrenching. Not one of them exemplified the optimism and excitement they had shared the night before.

None of them had gotten more than a few hours of sleep the previous night. Vicky hadn't gone to sleep until long after midnight, and she was already awake when Erica tapped her on the shoulder before six o'clock.

Except for the contractors, Keith and Alvin, who were used to construction work, the other men and women who had helped remove the debris of the old church and pour concrete foundations for the new building slumped over their plates. Every move they made brought a grimace of pain to their faces. Although he had felt a twinge of pain, following his surgeon's advice, Chad hadn't done any lifting, but he had already worn holes in one pair of gloves, and he showed Vicky the blisters he had on two of his fingers. And his day hadn't been as difficult as many of the others for he had taken Vicky shopping.

Erica decided that she needed to be cooking

all day so Floyd had asked Chad and Vicky to go to the market in Saint-Marc and buy any fruit and vegetables they would need for a few days. Pierre smilingly agreed to go along as their interpreter.

At his direction they had visited three markets buying mangoes, papayas, avocados, oranges, tangelos, sweet potatoes and shallots. Vicky had hesitated but finally bought two pumpkins, wondering if she and Erica could possibly come up with some kind of pumpkin pies. She had also bought some typically Haitian products that Erica needed for the native dishes she intended to prepare.

They purchased a dozen loaves of fresh bread from a bakery, and Erica sliced half of the bread right away to serve with the canned beef stew she had warmed for their lunches. And although it had taken most of the morning to bake, she had baked three box cakes in the antiquated pans they'd found in the cabinets which they had scrubbed and sanitized. Erica's face expressed complete astonishment when she surveyed the tables at the end of the meal.

"I thought surely there would be some cake left for an afternoon snack," she confided to Vicky as they carried the empty pans back to the kitchen.

"Let's serve potato chips and Kool-Aid for their snack."

"You take care of it when it's time, and I'll start making a pot of chili with the fresh meat you bought." She sniffed the red peppers. "Wow! That opened up my sinuses!"

"Shall I cut up some of the fruit into a salad?"

"Yes. As soon as I have the chili simmering, I'll stir up several boxes of corn bread. With the small oven and its low temperature, I can only make one pan of bread at a time."

Although the first few days were difficult, their bodies acclimated to the rigorous regimen. The volunteers worked all day and slept well each night. Chad noticed that everyone was so immersed in the work at hand that they didn't tell time by the calendar but by the progress they were making on the church.

After the nightly devotional, Chad and Vicky always walked to the beach. Most of the time, they were accompanied by some of the others, who found it more pleasant to bathe in the ocean than in the small shower stall which provided only a trickle of water most of the time. Chad was frustrated that he and Vicky couldn't find time to be alone. Would he have to wait until they returned to the States to tell her what was in his heart?

Chapter Seventeen

On a Saturday fifteen days from the time they'd arrived in Haiti, Chad climbed down from a ladder and laid aside a paintbrush. La Peti Ville again had a place to worship. He stood back and admired the church's original sign he had just nailed in place—one of the few things not destroyed by the hurricane. He had used the brush to touch up a few of the spots on the sign he'd scarred when hanging it.

L'église évangélique

Pausing for a rest between kitchen tasks, Vicky stopped by to compliment Chad on his work.

"Evangelical Church," she read. "You guys have done an excellent job. I can't wait until tomorrow when they have the dedication service."

"Have you and Erica put the finishing touches

on the dinner we're going to share with the whole congregation?"

"We'll see." She arched her eyebrows and shook her head. "Erica is determined to serve some Haitian food. I argued that the way we prepare their dishes probably won't look or taste the same as if the natives had prepared them. But we're going to have Labouyi Banann and Conch Lambi whether we want them or not."

Chad laughed richly. "Will you tell me what the ingredients are so I'll know if I want to eat them?"

"Labouyi Banann is sort of like a pudding. It's made of bananas and plantains with milk and lots of spices. It's good. And the Conch Lambi is made from shelled conch, which took a lot of work to clean and skin. Then we added onions, shallots, tomatoes and spices. I think our people will like the different dishes, but I'm convinced the Haitians would have preferred pizza or hamburgers. Erica and I compromised, though. We still have quite a few potato chips, boxes of cookies and packages of Kool-Aid and that's going to be dessert for everybody."

"I've missed talking to you," he said, and she nodded understandingly.

"It won't be much longer until we're home and we can talk as often as we want to."

"I feel as if I've been here half of my life," he said.

"I understand that. Time could have been standing still as far as I'm concerned. Do you realize that we haven't heard a newscast or a weather report for two weeks?"

"And strange as it seems, I haven't even missed it."

Chad's gaze traveled over her face and searched her eyes and she felt wrapped in invisible warmth. He reached for her hand, and her pulses suddenly leaped with excitement. Fearing her reaction if she stayed any longer, Vicky turned away. "I must go help Erica. We'll have supper before long."

The bell had been salvaged when the hurricane struck, and Alvin Cross had hung it in the new steeple the day before. The volunteers were almost as excited as the Haitians when Pierre rang the bell calling the faithful to worship the next morning. The Americans were given a place of honor in the front of the church, which meant that many Haitians had to stand.

Which also meant that the church was too small, Vicky suggested to Floyd quietly, although he assured her that the normal congregation wasn't usually so large. "Many friends and relatives from other villages have come for the dedication of the church," he whispered.

Vicky listened to the pianist's spirited rendition of familiar songs while the worshippers settled into the available pews or stood around the walls. Again she had reason to be proud of Chad—if it hadn't been for him, there wouldn't have been any musical accompaniment.

A week earlier when Chad learned from Floyd that the church's piano had been destroyed, he insisted on replacing it. Pierre borrowed a truck from the owner of a sugar plantation a few miles away to take Floyd and Chad to Port-au-Prince. A used spinet piano was found, purchased and installed in the completed church. The pastor's wife proved to be a fairly good musician, and Vicky thanked God silently that He had given Chad the opportunity to use his money to provide for the village.

Most of the volunteers sang with the congregation, singing in English for the hymns were familiar ones. Vicky was content to sit and listen to the soft cadences of the Haitian language as the natives swayed to the sound of the music, some of the young women as supple and graceful as palm trees stirring in the wind.

The pastor stood behind a beautifully crafted podium that Keith Cross had finished yesterday. It was amazing how God had taken the talents of all the volunteers and blended them together to provide this building. Vicky could only pick up a word or two of the pastor's message, but she worshipped as readily as if she understood every word. The spirit of God was present, making all of them as one people.

In their last nightly get-together, Floyd asked for individual impressions of their mission involvement. Smith Baxter, with a roguish look at his wife, said jokingly, "Today was the best day we've had. I've never been hugged and kissed by so many women in my life—at least not in one day."

Everyone laughed at his comment for the natives had included the Americans in their normal customs of worship—all of which were more emotional and jubilant than the stateside people had experienced.

"How many of you would volunteer for another mission tour?" Floyd asked.

As one, all of the hands were lifted.

"It's especially meaningful for me," Chad said. "I came here expecting direction for my life, and I've received it. I'm not ready to share details with you right now, but this tour has changed my life. In fact *I* don't know all of the details, but God has shown the next two or three steps I'm to take. That's enough for now."

After the meeting Chad and Vicky started

toward the beach. He was pleased that everyone else had decided to pack and get ready for their return trip to Port-au-Prince the next day, for he wanted to talk to Vicky alone. He took her hand as they strolled, savoring the breeze from the ocean.

"It's going to be different going back to Columbus and the hot, humid weather after we've been here for over two weeks," Vicky said.

"When Floyd went to his office in Port-au-Prince yesterday, he had emails concerning the weather. Most of the Midwest is having extremely hot temperatures."

They walked silently until they sighted the ocean. They paused to take in the beauty of the scene as they always did. Vicky thought she could become addicted to living in a place like this. The breeze was balmy, and the moon just peeping over the horizon made the spot seem like a fairyland.

"I believe I've found my mission," Chad said, interrupting her thoughts.

"In Haiti?" Vicky questioned with a sense of apprehension. Would his mission make a difference in their relationship?

"It's started here, but I'll not know what I can do until I'm home. I want to use the proceeds from my biography to set up a foundation to provide internet service for remote mission stations around the world. Think what it would mean to this orphanage if those kids could access the internet for their studies. It will probably involve a lot of red tape, but it must be feasible or I wouldn't feel so strongly that this is what God wants me to do."

"It will be a big project!"

"That's true. I'd need a lot of expert help, but I do understand the basics of what would be involved to provide internet coverage. Along with my engineering degree, I have a minor in computer science so I'm not a novice in the field. What do you think?"

"It would be a great blessing to many people. You could probably get direction through the mission board of our denomination."

"I've worked this all out in my mind as I've been working and walking along the beaches. If I can buy Grace's house, I'll set up my office in the front room to the right of the stairway and use the rest for my home."

"You think she'll sell to you?"

"I think so when I tell her that I don't intend to live there alone." They were at the edge of the water now and the soft waves brushed the tips of their shoes. Chad had rehearsed over and over in his mind how to propose to Vicky. He was tongue-tied now and he wondered if he would botch the whole thing.

"I suppose you only think of me as a friend, and your former experiences may not have prepared you to love again." Her lips parted in surprise, and Chad gulped, but he finally found the courage to complete what he'd started to say. "But I hope someday you will learn to love me as much as I love you, and become my wife to share my home and vision."

So he did love her! Vicky's pulses leaped with excitement, but she was determined to make Chad see her as she was.

"But I'm not the kind of person you need for a wife. You need someone who is educated like you and Perry and Lorene. I felt so stupid when they were in Columbus and we had dinner together. I didn't know anything to say to them."

"You wouldn't feel that way if you knew Lorene and Perry better. But if that's the only barrier to our happiness, you've already taken the right step by enrolling in OSU to complete your education. But I don't want to wait until you've graduated to get married."

Vicky turned and faced him squarely, holding his gaze with her own. "I've known since Christmas that what I *thought* was friendship for you is really love."

He pulled her toward him, but she held him at arm's length. "Let me finish. Before I give you an answer, we need to have an understanding about my relationship with Damon. I know now that my reaction to both him and Allen Chambers was a physical thing, not the deep, inner feeling that I have for you. But you must understand that Damon and I didn't have an 'affair,' as the common term seems to be. If I marry you, I'll be coming to you with a pure body and heart. You must believe that."

"When you first told me about him, the possibility flitted through my mind, but since I've come to know you so well, there has never been any doubt in my mind. So if that's all that stood in the way, is your answer yes?"

"Yes. Yes. Yes."

As though Vicky's words released him, Chad picked her up in his arms and swung her around and around, laughing into her eyes.

"Put me down," she said, "You're making me dizzy."

He set her feet on the ground, but still held her tightly in his arms. "You've made me dizzy, too. Dizzy with love for you. Ah, Vicky, my love, we're going to have a wonderful life together. When will you marry me?"

"A month from today," she promised, "if we can get your widely scattered family gathered by then. And if Mom can plan a wedding in such a short time," she qualified.

"No ifs about it. We're getting married on

that day. Let's make a deal—you plan the wedding the way you want it. I'll plan the honeymoon."

"Have you decided where we'll go?"

"To Hawaii. When you told me you'd love to go there, I decided it would be the place for our honeymoon."

His lips came coaxingly down on hers and Vicky returned his kiss. For a moment the thought of Chad's fortune compared to her lack of wealth filtered through Vicky's mind. But she must stop looking for excuses. They wanted each other, and she believed that their marriage was God's will for their lives. But as he kissed her again, Vicky's optimism faded slightly and she marveled that a man like Chad had chosen her.

Epilogue

Five years later Chad again spent the night in OSU Medical Center, but this time Vicky was the one in bed. She had been in labor most of the night and Chad stayed in the room with her, helping her through the contractions as he'd been taught in prenatal classes. When it was time for delivery, Chad followed Vicky to the delivery room and held her hand until the birth of their son—Trevor Saunders Reece. Tears blinding his eyes, he bent to kiss Vicky and rushed out of the room to a nearby waiting area where his parents, Vicky's parents, Perry, Lorene and Amy waited.

"She's all right. The doctor said she had an easy delivery, but it was sure hard on me. The baby's perfect but he was crying when I left the room, so I have to hurry back. I'll let you know when she's back in the room."

He couldn't understand why all the adults laughed at him. They just didn't realize what he'd gone through.

"We'll only say hello to Vicky and see the baby for a few minutes," Mrs. Reece said, "then go to the hotel."

"Same here," Perry said. "You and Vicky both need to rest tonight."

"Chad, we can stay with Vicky while you have dinner with your family," Rachel said. "She'll be sleeping anyway."

After all of the family had gone, Chad sat by his son's bassinet, listening to Vicky's quiet breathing. His thoughts turned to the past five years and the happiness he had found.

His biography had been a bestseller, and the proceeds from it—and the following movie—had netted enough to establish Reece Enterprises. The foundation was set up to use his money for philanthropic needs for years to come. internet services had already been installed in two Haitian villages, and Chad had flown to several Latin American countries to survey other potential projects.

He and Vicky had settled comfortably into Grace's home, which she had sold to them prior to their marriage. She enjoyed living in Texas near her family, but every summer she came to spend two weeks in her ancestral home.

Tears stung Chad's eyes and he knelt by his chair. Why had God singled him out to be the one to carry the Gospel into Latin American countries via the internet? He didn't know, but he was grateful that God had not only called him, but that he'd had the courage to follow.

Through the years he had often wondered about Oliver. He prayed every day that he would meet him again to let him know that the message he had delivered to Chad had set his feet on the right path.

"One day at a time, Lord, that's all I'm asking. Thank you from the depth of my heart for working Your will in my life."

Vicky stirred and he hurried to her bed to see if she needed anything, but she was asleep. He bent and kissed her, and she smiled slightly. He returned to his chair, stopping beside Trevor's bed long enough to touch the tiny cheek with his lips. Sighing, Chad stretched out in the lounge chair. He hoped sleep would come soon. He'd had a hard day.

* * * * *

Dear Reader,

My book *Love at Last,* was published in 2002. In that book, Lorene Harvey had given her baby up for adoption without telling his father, Perry Saunders. But they meet again twenty years later. Near the end of the book, Lorene and Perry encounter their son, Chad Reece, and he has no idea that they are his biological parents. Because they didn't want to disrupt his happy life, Lorene and Perry concealed their relationship to him.

Two years ago my editor and I agreed upon a sequel to *Love at Last,* with Chad as the hero and Vicky Lanham of *Second Chance Love* as the heroine.

A Husband for All Seasons brings Chad and Vicky together during tragic circumstances when his true parentage is revealed. As Vicky helps Chad deal with the news that changes his life forever, she also wrestles with her own unhappy past.

I pray that your own faith will be renewed as you read the heart-wrenching incidents that increase Chad's and Vicky's faith.

Irene B. Brand

Questions for Discussion

1. Discuss Chad's reaction to his traumatic physical injury and his uncertain future. Do you think his reaction was realistic? What would you have done in his place? Have you ever had something traumatic happen that changed your life? Who did you turn to for help?

2. Consider the fact that Chad had never wanted to know anything about his biological parents. Do you feel his anger toward his adoptive parents for keeping Lorene and Perry's connection to him secret was justified?

3. Compare Chad's situation to someone you know who has been adopted. Were they interested in learning about their biological parents? Why are some people determined to know about their roots, while it never matters to others? If you were in Chad's position, would you have wanted to know?

4. Consider Vicky's embarrassment and depression over her two heartbreaks. Do you feel that she overreacted to the situations because she was so young? Have your teen-

age romances had an impact on your adult life? How?

5. Read Acts 16: 6–10. It's a common saying that "when God closes one door, He opens another." Have you found this true in your life? How strong was your faith during that time? Did you blame God for your problems?

6. Have you ever been involved in a romance that seemed perfect, only to be rejected by the one you loved? Did love come to you again and you could see God's wisdom in preventing you from marrying the first person?

7. Does it seem unusual that Stewart and Betty Reece easily accepted Chad's biological parents and allowed them to share in his life? How have adoptive parents you've known dealt with their children wanting to find their biological parents?

8. Vicky felt that she had received God's call to devote her life to full-time Christian service. She had made a vow/promise and had failed to keep it. When God singles out individuals for special service, can that person ever be content spiritually if they don't

follow God's will for their lives? Has God ever given you a special opportunity to do His work? Did you readily answer the call or did you resent God's interference?

9. How significant is the fleeting appearance of Oliver in Chad's life? Do you believe that God sends people into our lives to point us in the direction He wants us to go?

10. At what point in the book do you believe that Chad knew he loved Vicky? And when did she realize that Chad was no longer a platonic friend but that she was falling in love with him? After her previous love interests, did she have reason to fear becoming too close to Chad?

11. Did Chad make the right decision in allowing his biography to be written and to have a movie made of his life? If you walked in his shoes, how would you have invested your millions to further the kingdom of God?

12. How did reading this book influence your personal walk with God?

REQUEST YOUR FREE BOOKS!
2 FREE RIVETING INSPIRATIONAL NOVELS PLUS 2 FREE MYSTERY GIFTS

YES! Please send me 2 FREE Love Inspired® Suspense novels and my 2 FREE mystery gifts (gifts are worth about $10). After receiving them, if I don't wish to receive any more books, I can return the shipping statement marked "cancel." If I don't cancel, I will receive 4 brand-new novels every month and be billed just $4.74 per book in the U.S. or $5.24 per book in Canada. That's a savings of at least 21% off the cover price. It's quite a bargain! Shipping and handling is just 50¢ per book in the U.S. and 75¢ per book in Canada.* I understand that accepting the 2 free books and gifts places me under no obligation to buy anything. I can always return a shipment and cancel at any time. Even if I never buy another book, the two free books and gifts are mine to keep forever.

123/323 IDN F5AN

Name _____ (PLEASE PRINT)

Address _____ Apt. #

City _____ State/Prov. _____ Zip/Postal Code

Signature (if under 18, a parent or guardian must sign)

Mail to the **Harlequin® Reader Service:**
IN U.S.A.: P.O. Box 1867, Buffalo, NY 14240-1867
IN CANADA: P.O. Box 609, Fort Erie, Ontario L2A 5X3

**Are you a current subscriber to Love Inspired Suspense books
and want to receive the larger-print edition?
Call 1-800-873-8635 or visit www.ReaderService.com.**

* Terms and prices subject to change without notice. Prices do not include applicable taxes. Sales tax applicable in N.Y. Canadian residents will be charged applicable taxes. Offer not valid in Quebec. This offer is limited to one order per household. Not valid for current subscribers to Love Inspired Suspense books. All orders subject to credit approval. Credit or debit balances in a customer's account(s) may be offset by any other outstanding balance owed by or to the customer. Please allow 4 to 6 weeks for delivery. Offer available while quantities last.

Your Privacy—The Harlequin® Reader Service is committed to protecting your privacy. Our Privacy Policy is available online at www.ReaderService.com or upon request from the Harlequin Reader Service.
We make a portion of our mailing list available to reputable third parties that offer products we believe may interest you. If you prefer that we not exchange your name with third parties, or if you wish to clarify or modify your communication preferences, please visit us at www.ReaderService.com/consumerschoice or write to us at Harlequin Reader Service Preference Service, P.O. Box 9062, Buffalo, NY 14269. Include your complete name and address.

LISDIR13R

REQUEST YOUR FREE BOOKS!

2 FREE INSPIRATIONAL NOVELS
PLUS 2
FREE
MYSTERY GIFTS

Love Inspired
HISTORICAL
INSPIRATIONAL HISTORICAL ROMANCE